# HACKED

The Secret of Secrets, Book 1

# HACKED

The Secret of Secrets, Book 1

Stephanie Connelley
WORLTON

Spring Canyon
MEDIA

ISBN-13: 978-0-9914589-4-3

Published by Spring Canyon Media
Herriman, Utah

Cover design and photography © 2015 Spring Canyon
Media. All rights reserved.

To my amazing introverted "computer geek" friends, thank you for sharing your friendship and your expertise with me. I have a feeling I've only begun to scratch the surface of your knowledge and experience.

# CHAPTER ONE

I've got secrets.

I know what you're thinking. Everybody has secrets. Well, sure. I suppose. But the secrets that keep me up at night are a lot bigger than the little hit-and-run I had when I was sixteen. Or even the kiss I shared with uber-geek Todd behind the marching band's bus. No, my secrets are the real deal. The kind that keep me looking over my shoulder and checking under my car. The kind I never signed up for and would do anything to get rid of. Society-altering, top-secret secrets.

It was well past normal business hours when my boss summoned me to his office. The fluorescent overhead lighting buzzed in the silence of the nearly empty building as I logged out of my workstation and made my way down the long stretch of cubicles. Most everyone else had gone home for the day, but I'd been onto something big for a couple of weeks and didn't like the idea of being dragged away from it. It didn't hurt that I had nothing to go home to. Which, most of the time was perfectly fine with me. I liked being alone almost as much as I liked checking off boxes and completing tasks.

Like everything in my boss's office, the hard chair he offered me was the finest example of government-issued boring. The air hung with the stagnancy of a mosquito infested pond.

"Miss Perry." Mr. Kravitsch's eye twitched behind his spectacles. Gray hair rimmed his head, creating a halo around his shiny skull. Dark, heavy bags hung under his eyes and his mouth was perpetually drawn down. "As you know, it's our objective to maintain the utmost degree of security for our government, our country, and our employees." The deep creases that bracketed his mouth stretched like a marionette when he talked.

I nodded. "Yes, sir." Confidentiality clauses and security screenings were something I'd grown quite familiar with. They'd been part of my daily protocol since being recruited from MIT to be a security analyst for the NSA.

"You have proven to be a most valuable asset to our country." The corners of his mouth turned up into the briefest hint of a smile, revealing a touch of his coffee stained teeth and a glimpse of personality from the otherwise dry man. A half second later, he returned to his typical rigidness. The permanent furrow in his brow intensified. "Your help in infiltrating networks, thus finding and removing sensitive government data from our enemies has been priceless. Your dedication to protecting our country's top defense contractors has been recognized at the highest levels. Our nation is undoubtedly in your debt."

With the exception of a computer monitor and keyboard, the thick wooden desktop was barren. I scanned the room and found it, too, was remarkably void of any decor, personal or otherwise.

"Thank you, sir." I nodded again, hoping he'd bring up 43M, the case I'd been so heavily involved in for the last several weeks. It had kept me late at the office for the past several nights, including this one. In a world of plastic money and digital banking, POS hacks – meaning point of sale – were constantly gaining frequency. Credit consumers were continually at risk of having their data stolen in one way or another. 43M was just such a breach. The coding had infected gas station terminals across the U.S. and, without the help of a physical card skimmer, successfully siphoned data and made charges to millions of consumer accounts. By adding one percent to every transaction, the hacker had been able to skim just over forty-three million dollars from unsuspecting credit card users in a single week.

I sat tall in my seat. Figuring out how the breach was pulled off had been the easy part. The challenge was figuring out who was behind it, especially given the hacker's apparent self-control. After just seven days, he pulled out of the systems and deleted all evidence that he'd been there . . . or so he thought. It had been my task to discover otherwise.

I folded my arms confidently across my chest. All my extra hours in the office hadn't gone unnoticed. Perhaps a raise was in my future.

"But . . ." Kravitsch cleared his throat. "Even when we do everything right," he glared at me, "sometimes things go wrong."

I shifted in my chair. Go wrong? What was he talking about? I'd followed every protocol, my code was always bug-free and performed exactly as intended, and, as the only female on an otherwise male team, my analytical skills and attention to detail were virtually unmatched. If he was implying that I'd done something wrong, he was mistaken. I was thorough and maybe even obsessive about getting things right. I could detect abnormalities in cyberspace better than any of my coworkers.

"Your workstation, including your laptop and cell phone are being wiped as we speak. Andre has taken the liberty of removing any items from your purse that might connect you back to this office."

I didn't have time to ask questions before a large man – presumably Andre – walked through the door with my handbag. "This is it, sir." His dark hair was knotted back, forming a ball just above the nape of his almost non-existent neck. The collar of his shirt stretched to contain his large deltoid and trapezius muscles. He dropped a handful of my personal effects in front of Kravitsch.

A tube of Pina Coloda lip balm rolled past the half-full carton of spearmint gum. Andre slammed his palm over it to keep it from rolling off the desk.

"What in the . . ." I started to ask as Kravitsch sorted my driver's license, credit cards, and car keys from the mix of other personal items. My body went rigid and my lower lip trembled.

"I'm going to need your employee badge as well," he said.

I drew a protective hand to the badge hanging around my neck. "I don't understand," I said. My hand shook as I pressed the lanyard to my chest.

"We do our utmost to protect our assets," Kravitsch said as he waggled an expectant finger in front of my badge. The room seemed to be spinning as I tried to process his words. My chest pressed in on itself. I forced myself to take a breath. And then another one.

Hesitantly I slid the chain over my head. He greedily snagged it from my grip then added it to the pile with my driver's license and credit cards. Looking over the rest of my personal items tersely, he pushed them aside and drew a manila envelope out of his top drawer. "There is a car waiting for you downstairs." He said each word slowly and clearly. "Andre will walk you out. Don't open this" – he raised the envelope – "until the driver tells you it's safe."

Andre took the envelope then handed it to me along with my newly empty purse.

"Last time I checked, improper search and seizure was against the law." I felt the fire in my cheeks and the vibrato in my voice. My red-headed temper was something only my family got to witness, but questioning my professional integrity and fingering through my stuff was too much. I smashed my lips together and tried to calm the volcano boiling in my chest.

"Like I said before," Kravitsch said, his voice as calm as mine was wild, "it is our mission to keep our country and our employees safe. Please keep your voice down and go with Andre."

"Go where with Andre?" I growled through clenched teeth. "Where is he taking me? And why do I need a driver?" I clenched my fists and drew a deep breath. "My car is in the parking garage. I can drive myself home." I reached to retrieve my keys off his desk as I stood.

"Perry" – Kravitsch pinned a definitive finger on top of my MIT keychain, preventing me from taking it. "I don't think you understand."

"I understand perfectly." My anger erupted as brightly as the red ponytail on the back of my head. "You're firing me. What I don't understand" – I slammed the palms of my hands down on his desk, barely aware of the manila envelope as it fell to the floor. – "is what I did to deserve this. I'm good at my job. I work hard, I stay late. I've never once breached protocol. If you've got a security leak, Mr. Kravitsch, it's not me!"

"Samantha." Kravitsch stood and looked me in the eye. It was the first time he'd ever used my first name. "You're not being fired."

"I'm not being fired?" I swallowed hard, but didn't break eye contact. "Then would you please explain what in the world is going on?"

"You may have been compromised," he said as nonchalantly as if he'd just ordered a bowl of pasta off a take-out menu. "We believe your role in one of our recent cases may be known."

"What are you talking about? I don't understand." Numbers and code from my latest projects ran through my mind. My code was tight. How could I be compromised? He had to be wrong.

"You're being relocated. The details are in the packet." He nodded at the envelope at my feet. "When you get to your destination, you'll receive further instruction."

I slid back into the chair and perched my head in my hands. "Is this some sort of witness protection plan?"

"In the sense that we need you to lay low for a while, sort-of. But really, it's just a safety measure until we can close up the threat. Think of it as a temporary relocation."

"Temporary?" My mind was busily trying to connect the dots. Compromised. Relocating. Temporary.

He nodded.

"So, when do I leave?" I pulled my cardigan around my torso, twisting it tightly as the unwelcome reality washed over me.

"You'll go straight to the airport from here." He sat back down.

"You can't expect me to just up and go. How will I get my stuff?"

Kravitsch tapped on his keyboard then spun his monitor around so I could see it. "There's not much left to grab," he said, pointing to the screen. I watched flames dance across the computer monitor from what appeared to be a security camera feed. The blaze roared up a staircase and lurched its way through the entire second story of the building. A burst blew out one of the windows, and that's when recognition hit me.

"That's not real. That can't be real." I scooted to the edge of my chair to get a better view. Kravitsch punched a few keys and the screen switched over to a live-news feed. A news anchor stood at the base of the apartment building, reporting live about a suspected gas explosion. I leaned in close enough to see the numbers that hung over what used to be a front door. 17-B. My address.

Words scrolled over the bottom of the screen, officially classifying the fire as a gas explosion. Smaller words stated that authorities were searching for survivors. "What if I hadn't been working late?" The words stammered past my lips. "And what about my neighbors?" I thought about the little girl with golden braids who lived in the apartment below mine. And the old guy next door. Somehow, I didn't know their names. Why did I not know their names? Suddenly I wished I'd been a better neighbor.

"Don't worry," Kravitsch said nonchalantly. "I'm sure they're fine."

Though I didn't understand his sense of calm, I was starting to get a feeling for the weight of the situation and Kravitsch's urgency about it.

I picked the envelope up off the ground and tucked it into my empty purse. I then rescued my lip balm and pack of gum off Kravitsch's desk, and drew in the biggest breath I could muster as I stood. "Can I call my parents before I go?" I pointed to my cell phone as I imagined them seeing the news unfold on their T.V. at home.

"No." Shaking his head, Kravitsch clamped his hand over my phone and scooted it out of my reach. "It's better that they don't know."

The knot in my chest became suffocating. How could I allow my parents to think I was dead?

"Perry," Kravitsch said as I followed Andre toward the door, "this is just temporary. As soon as we get it worked out, we'll bring you back to Maryland. If you keep your head down and be smart, everything will be okay." He almost sounded human. And I almost took comfort in his words until he added three more: "Trust no one."

I took one last look at the remains of my identity strewn across Kravitsch's desk, then looked up at him haltingly. This wasn't what I'd signed up for. Running and hiding and pretending weren't things in my job description. I was a cyber-geek, plain and simple. I worked on computers and, when necessary, I spoke nerd to other nerds. That was about as adventurous as I got. I didn't want this life. I was a quiet, keep-to-myself, check-the-boxes kind of girl, not some adrenaline-junkie secret agent.

The sun sank over the Maryland horizon as Andre ushered me into the back of a black Chevy Tahoe. There were two leather bucket seats. I slid into the one closest to me on the passenger side of the SUV, assuring a clear view of the driver. The large-shouldered man wore his hair buzzed short. A wire twisted its way out of his broad collar and into his ear. His eyes were glued to his windshield and both of his hands were squared on the steering wheel.

Andre made sure my door was secure then climbed in the seat in front of me.

A tree shaped silhouette hung from the rearview mirror, filling the car with the scent of artificial pine. It laced with the musky smell of leather seats and the burly scent of man, tickling my nose. The combination might have been welcome had it represented a date or something less dramatic than being rushed away from everything that was comfortable in my life.

Scratching the end of my nose, I turned toward the dark window. Heavy tinting blocked any sign of life on the outside of the car. It was so dark, I'm certain the inside of the car would've appeared to be night time even if it had been the middle of the day.

"Can I have a light back here?" I asked the men in the front seat as I pulled the manila envelope out of my purse and dumped its contents on the seat beside me. Neither one of them responded. "Please?" I added with a softer tone.

"I'm sorry." Andre's deep voice cut in staccatoed beats through the darkness. "We must keep cover." He kept his eyes straight ahead.

Five, I counted to myself, sucking in as much air as my lungs could handle. The smell of leather mixed with artificial pine filled my nostrils. Four. I pushed the air – in small, almost rhythmic motions – out of my chest. Three. I drew in another long, purposeful breath. Two. I let it out: the pine scent, the musky leather, and the anxious knot in my chest. One. In again. Deep. Thoughtful. Relaxing.

Letting my eyes adjust to the darkness, I picked up the paperclipped pile that had fallen out of the envelope, and pulled it close to my eyes. A plane ticket lay on the top of the neatly stacked papers. I squinted in the darkness to decipher the destination —one way to the Salt Lake City International Airport. Under the ticket was a crisp, new passport, a small bundle of cash, a single credit card, and a driver's license.

I pulled the driver's license out of the bundle and examined it. According to the information on the front of the card I was a resident of Utah with brown hair and brown eyes, a B-level restriction that meant I was required to wear corrective lenses when driving, and my name was Ginger Alston.

*Ginger?* Seriously? I wanted to laugh out loud. Or cry. The American government – an agency with unlimited resources – couldn't do better than a stripper name? Of course, even if I could pass as a Ginger without snickering every time someone said my name, none of the other information was true either. How was I supposed to pass through airport security when my red hair and blue eyes clearly didn't match the girl pictured on my new ID? My stomach dropped at the realization. More than my name had to change.

The driver stopped his vehicle in front of a security station, flashed a card through the window, then drove into a dimly lit parking garage. Pulling to a stop in a secluded corner, he shut the engine off. There wasn't a single other car anywhere to be seen.

Andre stepped out, walked back to my door, and pulled it open. Nodding toward a tiny Asian woman who'd seemingly appeared out of nowhere, he coaxed me out with a wave of his hand.

He pushed the car door closed, making barely a sound in the empty garage, then, crossing his arms over his chest, perched himself against the side of the car.

The little lady turned away and started walking. Andre raised his chin in her direction, a sign that I assumed meant I was supposed to follow her. I silenced the plethora of questions I had and trailed behind her shadow down a long, dark hallway. My stomach was in knots, anticipating the moment she might reconnect with those kung-fu skills that had allowed her to appear out of nowhere.

Gratefully, she didn't open up any ninja moves on me before reaching the end of the hallway. I'd have never stood a chance against her. Or anyone for that matter. I was in way over my head.

There was only one door at the end of the hall. A large, metal one. The little lady pulled it open effortlessly. It slammed heavily behind us before the overhead lights flickered on.

A single salon chair sat in the stark room behind a floor to ceiling mirror. Beside the mirror hung the same photoshopped image of me that they'd used for my new ID. Brown haired, brown eyed me. I wasn't sure I liked the look – it was far less conservative than I was comfortable with – but the urgency with which Kravitsch ushered me out of the office indicated that it was necessary.

The little ninja-lady motioned me to sit and I didn't dare argue. She slid the hair tie off my ponytail, freeing my hair to flow down past the middle of my back. She drew a comb through the tangles, mumbling something in her native tongue, then grabbed her sheers and spun the chair so my back was to the mirror.

The muscles in my jaw tightened as I heard the scissors claim their first chunk of hair. I gripped the armrests and focused on steadying my emotions. How had I been compromised?

An hour later, eight inches of natural red curls scattered over the floor. Kung-fu lady instructed me to stand. "Gib me you swatter," she ordered.

"My sweater?"

"Yas. You swatter." She pointed to my cardigan.

Hesitantly, I slid the soft, brown cable knit off my shoulders and handed it to her.

"I put in trash where it belong."

I flinched in horror as she tossed it in the trash can. "But I love that sweater," I defended.

"It ugly," she said matter-of-factly. "Dis so blaw." She grabbed the collar of my white blouse and, without hesitation, unbuttoned the top two buttons. "So better." She played with my collar again, this time pulling the lapel edges outward.

"Now skirt and shoe." She pointed to my navy pleated skirt and simple black flats. "I get you better."

Not brave enough to argue with her, I slipped off my shoes and slithered out of my skirt while she opened a wardrobe closet and riffled through it.

"Here," she said, handing me a pair of black business pants and leopard print heals.

I shimmied into the skin-tight slacks, uncomfortable with how they hugged every curve of my lower body, then slid my foot into the three-inch heels. "I don't do heels very well." I eyed my discarded black flats, hoping she'd allow me some level of comfort.

"Den you learn." She looked me over then, with a nod of approval, turned me around to face the mirror. "You like?" She smiled at her work.

The girl in the mirror was pretty. Her short, blunt cut hair hung in loose, sassy curls just above her shoulders. Her lips were full and colored with a radiant shade of red that accentuated her deep brown eyes. Even the shoes were appealing. But she wasn't me.

Ninja-lady gave me about thirty-seconds to look myself over and then, without having fully processed the stranger staring back at me, I was back in the car.

The driver and Andre maintained complete silence for the drive. No music, no conversation, only the noise of the road beneath us. And, as far as I was concerned, that was a good thing. I didn't like small-talk, and I certainly didn't need a stranger to dig into my feelings. Especially since I hadn't even had time to form any, let alone process them.

Compromised. Transferred. New identity. I repeated the words over and over in my head as I stared at my reflection in the car window. Only it wasn't me. It was the newly invented me. The one where I sported a dark, shoulder length, blunt-cut bob and looked like I'd stepped out of a fashion magazine. The one where I was known as Ginger. Ugh. I silently repeated the name with disgust. Ginger snap. Ginger Spice. Ginger ale.

The driver dropped me at Dulles Airport and Andre escorted me through security with just enough time to board a red-eye to Salt Lake. Without luggage, we moved quickly through the terminal, stopping only briefly when I caught a glimpse of my burned-down apartment building on a recap of the nightly news. I wanted to mourn the loss of my identity, my family, my apartment, and the only life I'd ever known, but the thumping in my chest reminded me that I was on the run from some unknown threat. I didn't have time for a breakdown. Andre stood silently by my side until the moment I boarded the plane. Like a child I simply followed his lead, blindly trusting that the US government knew what it was doing.

As the plane lifted, the stress of my evening started closing in. I'd always been a numbers and patterns girl. I liked order and had never made even the most trivial of moves without a solid game plan. Spontaneity was not my forte.

My hands shook and my head pounded in almost the same rhythm as my heart. I looked around the cabin, taking inventory of everyone and everything around me. Not that I'd have known what to do had someone actually assaulted me. I was fit and healthy, but definitely not strong enough to fight anyone off –

especially in high heels. I'd made an investment in my brain, not my biceps, and for the first time in my life I questioned the wisdom of that choice.

I tightened my grip on the armrests and, pinching my eyes closed momentarily, focused on my breathing. In and out. In and out. In – *I hoped that Kravitsch's plan included placing someone on the plane who knew more about protecting me than I did* – and out. In – *if not, I'd have lost eight inches of hair and my favorite cardigan for nothing* – and out.

As soon as we reached altitude, I moved to an empty row of seats in the back of the cabin so I could have full view of the entire airplane.

My eyes were heavy, but the uncertainty of what stood before me wouldn't let me sleep. I'd lost control of my life. The government was calling all the shots now, not just in my professional life, but in the totality of who I was. I took comfort in Kravitsch's parting words. Not the part where he'd said to trust no one, because, frankly, there was no comfort to be found there. But the words before that. The ones where he said, "It's only temporary." I repeated the phrase over and over in my mind. "It's only temporary . . ."

# CHAPTER TWO

"Welcome to Salt Lake City," the captain announced when we touched down nearly four hours later. "Current local time is four-thirty-seven a.m. The temperature is a cool fifty-two degrees Fahrenheit with a projected high of sixty-eight this afternoon. The relative humidity is twenty-one percent with a one percent chance of showers. In other words, folks, it's gonna be a beautiful spring day along the Wasatch Front."

I unbuckled my seatbelt and waited for the plane to empty before I made my way up the aisle toward the exit. My heart pounded loudly in my chest and my hands were clammy as my anxiety grew. I had no idea what my next move was or how I was supposed to find out.

"Excuse me, ma'am," the flight attendant called as I passed her. "You forgot your luggage." She shoved the small carry-on into my arms before I could protest.

"But" – I looked down at the black backpack. I hadn't brought anything but my nearly empty purse with me, but this bag was clearly mine. Even if it hadn't had the name *Ginger Alston* printed on a large floral tag, I'd have recognized the bag anywhere. It was the one I'd carried all through college. Someone must have pulled it from my apartment before the explosion. Which meant . . . I didn't know what it meant. There were a lot of things I wanted it to mean, but after being awake for twenty-four hours straight, I didn't trust my judgment. My imagination was on overdrive. I needed to sleep before I started drawing unfounded conclusions.

"Thanks." Taking the bag, I bee-lined it down the jet bridge and into the nearest bathroom. When I was securely hidden inside a stall, I opened the top zipper. Stress and exhaustion had stolen my composure and I wasn't sure I could avoid a breakdown if I opened the mystery bag in public. I pulled out an envelope containing a set of keys and a note. My heart settled to a normal pace when I recognized Kravitsch's handwriting.

Following the instructions to parking lot C, row 14, I clicked the key fob and listened for a honking horn. Identifying the no-frills Honda Accord, I slid into the driver's seat and waited—as Kravitsch's instructions had indicated—for the built-in navigation system to load the coordinates for my pre-programmed destination.


Nearly forty miles south, I pulled into the parking lot of a condominium complex. I didn't see any springs as the city's name implied and not a whole lot of green either. Granted, I hadn't seen much of anything but asphalt and desert in my forty-mile drive, but at least the small town of Saratoga Springs appeared to have a few trees. And mountains. Beautiful ranges of tans and greens. It was a far cry from the lush landscape of the east coast, but for a short time I could handle anything. Probably. Maybe.

The GPS coordinates in the navigation system were very specific. Parking in the stall that the computerized voice indicated, I analyzed everything around me as I waited for my next set of instructions. After ten minutes nothing had surfaced. My stomach sank and panic began to settle in. Kravitsch wouldn't have brought me all this way to leave me hanging. Something had to have gone wrong.

My imagination cranked into gear. Maybe watching all those psychological thrillers in my teens hadn't been such a good idea. I gripped the steering wheel and tried to control my breathing. I counted down from ten only to realize that it wasn't working. My heart was racing. I needed air.

Against my intuition, I did a visual sweep of the parking lot. Two-dozen vehicles sat along the perimeter of the lot, edging up to a finely manicured lawn. About every fifth car, in the middle of the lawn, stood a small tree – maple, I think, though significantly smaller than the ones that I was used to seeing. Six buildings framed the area – three in front of me and three behind. Steep gables rose over the third-story of each matching building, capping the yellow-beige siding and tan-brick structures. Parking lights flickered overhead, confused by the soft light of early morning sun.

Confirming that there still weren't any other people out, I swept my eyes around again. Not another soul in sight. Grabbing my bags from the passenger seat, I secured my keys between my fingers like my college self-defense coach had taught and cautiously opened my door.

I stepped out of the car and sucked in the morning air. It took four breaths of the thin, dry air before any oxygen registered in my lungs. I began to pace. Forward, backward, then forward again. On the third pass I paused at my front bumper. Painted on the curb was the number twenty-three and the letter E.

I looked at the buildings clustered around me. Each one was identified by a giant letter. F and G were directly in front of me, which put E . . . right behind me. I turned abruptly and headed for the building.

I was aware of every movement and sound around me as I scaled the first set of stairs to the second floor.

There were two doors – one on either side of the landing. They were labeled with the numbers twenty-one and twenty-two. Still keeping tabs on my surroundings, I went back down to the sidewalk, walked around the building to the other side, and ascended back up to the second floor. Two brass numbers were affixed to the front of the door to the right. A two and a three.

I dug through my bag in hopes of finding a key, but didn't find anything. In desperation, I turned to my purse. Nothing. Folding my arms across my chest, I leaned back against the stucco wall and let out an exasperated sigh. I was about to head back to my car and shed some tears when I noticed a piece of glass was missing from the porch light. I moved in closer and rose up on my toes to get a better look.

A key. In the light. Though I hadn't expected Kravitsch to be so cliché, I didn't bother to wonder how it got there. I pulled it out and tested it in the lock.

Sun filtered through beige window coverings, dimly lighting the small apartment. A simple, dated kitchen welcomed me as I passed through the front door. Two wooden chairs were tucked under the edge of a small, lightly-stained kitchen table in the center of the space, and a stiff-looking sofa anchored the far side of the room. Other than a 40" TV, a purple accent wall, and a couple of purple pillows, the space was incredibly basic and boring.

Locking the door behind me, I secured both the deadbolt and the security lock, and slowly made my way around the apartment. It was a small, open concept space with one bedroom and a single bath. Simple and clean like a stock photo from a magazine.

I stepped into the bedroom, pulling the curtains just enough to let the morning light cast itself into the dungeon-like space. Like the living area, the bedroom was void of any hominess. It was a step up from the government grade of boring at the office, but not much. The queen-sized mattress had no head board and there wasn't a single picture on the wall. A purple bedspread sat on the foot of the bed, complete with a set of beige sheets – all still in their packaging. A cell phone lay on the bedroom dresser next to an NSA security badge with Ginger's photo and work credentials. I traced my fingers over the face of my new badge, still unsettled about my new reality, then pulled open the bedroom closet to access its contents.

Neatly pressed professional wear, jeans, and even work-out clothes all hung on simple metal hangers. They weren't really my style – the skirts were shorter, the pants tighter, and the blouses more revealing than I was used to – but I reconciled that I was supposed to be pretending to be someone that I wasn't, and for that purpose, they would do. Slipping out of the shirt I'd been wearing since the previous morning, I tossed it to the floor then pulled a purple t-shirt off its hanger and slid into it.

Exhausted and overwhelmed, I sat on the edge of the mattress and tried to absorb it all. Apparently

Ginger's favorite color was purple, her décor skills were boring, and her personal wardrobe style was loud and flirty.

*       *       *

*Keep your head on a swivel. Don't contact home. Don't leave your apartment until we give you the all clear.*

The anonymous texts appeared on Ginger's new phone that first day in Utah. The simple instructions were the only contact I had with the outside world and I didn't even know who they were from. No contact name. No identifiable number, but whoever "we" was, they were clearly in the know and communicating with me.

I spent the next few days holed up in my apartment, binge watching Netflix and reciting the texter's phrases while I waited for further instructions: *Keep your head on a swivel. Don't contact home.*

I was on edge and, for the first time in my life, I actually wanted to call my mom. The silence of my beige and purple one-room apartment was killing me. And so were the cupboards full of junk food that whoever set up my apartment had stashed. The Slim-Jim's and Poppin' Hot Jalapeño Doritos were clearly the work of a man. Probably a single one, with zero experience with girls. I'd have killed for a bowl of chowder or even a donut. Anything but the prepackaged testosterone food in my kitchen.

I flinched out of my reclining position on the couch when I heard a knocking sound on my door. Tucking my knees under me, I quickly turned the volume on the TV down, hoping whoever it was would think no one was home. "Keep your head on a swivel," I whispered quietly, sweeping my head around to take an inventory of the room. Every movement outside, every noise, every shadow on the wall had become a potential predator.

A second knock rapped on the door followed quickly by the doorbell. I swallowed back my imaginative fears and, though I normally would have just ignored an unexpected visitor, allowed my paranoia to slowly guide me across the room to the door.

"Friend or foe?" I silently asked myself as I peeked through the peephole. The perky young brunette with a baby on her hip certainly didn't look like a threat, but I wasn't about to take a chance. And I didn't want a friend. I watched the twenty-something lady fidget nervously, her messy ponytail bobbing loosely as she bounced her hip to adjust the baby's position. The small child could just be a diversion, I convinced myself as I held vigil on my side of the door. If someone was willing to blow up my apartment, who knew what lengths they'd go through to get to me.

I was cautiously aware of the slightest sounds inside and outside of my apartment as I watched the lady's every movement through the small glass hole. She said something to the baby, knocked one last time, then shrugged her shoulders and turned away. As she stepped away from the door, she passed a foil covered parcel from the same hand she'd been using to hold the baby, to her other one, then disappeared down the stairs.

Two hours later, the same scenario repeated itself. The third time she showed up, she had a man with her. This time he held the baby while she managed the package. When I didn't answer the door, they had a short conversation, ending with a shrug from the pony-tailed lady. She set the foil package on my doormat, took the baby from the man, then descended the stairs and disappeared from my view.

I dashed to the far side of my apartment, prepared for the foil package to blow my door down, or maybe the whole place. Ten minutes passed before I unburied my head from my arms, feeling like an idiot. Standing up from my squatted position in the corner, I traced the perimeter of the room while slowly making my way back to the door. I don't even know why I did that, other than that's what it seemed like the people in movies did. They also had guns. Why didn't I have a gun?

I pressed my eye to the peep hole. All clear. Cautiously I opened the door enough to view the package. It appeared to be a plate covered with foil. I touched it with the tip of my toe, as if having my foot blown off was any better than my arm.

Nothing happened.

I nudged the package a second time. Once again, it offered no response. Sweeping the area again with my eyes, I stooped down and turned the foil cover back.

Cookies. I'd had a panic attack over cookies? I'd officially become a freak. It was a good thing the government hadn't decided to give me a weapon. I was a ridiculous mess.

I snatched the plate and quickly retreated inside, locking the door tightly behind me.

The aroma of homemade chocolate chip cookies quickly filled my small apartment. A cutesy note was attached to the plate, introducing the couple as my down-stairs neighbors. The note identified them as Tiffanie, Mike, and baby Ian.

Wishing whoever had set up my apartment had left me a computer, I opened a search browser on my new phone. A quick public search rendered the information I sought. The flat below me was, indeed, rented out to one Michael F. Fredericks. He'd lived there for just over a year. Another search identified him as a graduate student at nearby Brigham Young University. And another rendered his marriage certificate to Tiffanie Lynn Sabastian. Baby Ian had been born last July at Timpanogos Regional Hospital. Everything I needed to know about them was literally at the tips of my fingers.

"Well, thank you, Tiffanie and Mike," I said out loud as I bit into a cookie. I took comfort in the normality of their lives and the fact that I hadn't even had to use my hacking skills to find information on them. Tiffanie's social media presence – an obsession, really – was an open book. She'd Instagrammed pretty much every detail of her life since meeting Mike in her singles ward – whatever that was – three years prior. I knew more about her from my ten-minute search than I did about my college roommates. Taking a second bite, I chewed it for about a half a second, then tossed the rest of the cookie in my mouth.

The purple walls started to close in around me again as I finished the last cookie on the plate. How long would I be forced to live in this violet prison? I wanted my simple, quiet, boring life back, but even more-so, I wanted to break the second two rules my unnamed texter had provided. But, if there was one thing I was not, it was a rule-breaker.

Then again, I wasn't really me anymore. I was Ginger. I gagged at the name.

Samantha was a rule-follower, but maybe Ginger wasn't.

I picked up Ginger's cell phone and headed to my – I mean, her – bedroom in search of shoes.

I may have lacked the physique of a body builder and I most definitely lacked the coordination of a dancer, but running was something I could manage. And I actually enjoyed it. It cleared my mind and allowed me to feel free. Two things I was in desperate need of.

I laced the brand-new shoes onto me feet then dialed my mom's number. My parents deserved to know what was going on. Images of flames shooting from my old apartment fogged my vision before I could finish dialing. If I called my parents would I be compromising their safety? Had I already put them at risk? I deleted the number and, still holding the phone in my hand, fell onto the bed.

*Don't call home and don't leave the apartment.* I analyzed everything those words could mean.

I yanked the shoes off my feet and threw them angrily across the room, then pressed my face into my pillow and, pretending I was too strong to cry, soothed myself with Kravitsch's words, "This is only temporary."

# Chapter Three

Temporary, as it turns out, is a very subjective term. In terms of a tattoo, temporary means about three weeks. If you're talking about a dental crown, perhaps the stretch goes as long as six months. But when it comes to being relocated by the government, temporary takes on a whole new level of ambiguity.

Seventeen weeks had passed since I'd become Ginger Alston. And, while one-hundred-and-nineteen days in the heat of the Utah desert had been doable, the twenty-five hundred hours I'd had to live with a name I utterly hated was its own special brand of torture.

"Excuse me, miss."

I flinched backward, bumping my shoulder into my car door as I stumbled in my three-inch heels. As had become my habit, I'd done a visual sweep of the area before shutting off my engine and stepping into the parking lot. I thought it had been empty. The man's unexpected presence caught me off guard. My heart raced as I turned toward him.

"Sorry to bother you," the man continued, as if he hadn't noticed my jumpiness. Talking to strangers had never been my thing, but since being thrust into my fake life I'd become even more introverted. Four months of constantly being on guard had morphed my already anti-social tendencies into something near paranoia. Everybody had become a potential threat.

With feigned confidence I turned to look at him. He wore a pair of dark jeans, not the kind that sagged low and baggy, but the kind that were fitted more around the waistline. They were clean and almost looked like he'd pressed every wrinkle out of them. His cotton t-shirt, a smooth heather gray, was also clean and not just wrinkle free, but graphic free as well. Classy. Mature, even. It hung loosely over his chest, but not loosely enough to hide the shadowed ridgelines of his toned abs and chest. My eyes affixed themselves to the size of his arms before I ever made it to his face. The set of finely toned biceps pressed tightly against his t-shirt sleeves, stretching the cotton like a softball emerging from a canvas.

I snapped back to reality. Everybody was a potential threat. If he'd wanted to, those arms could have already torn me to shreds.

I peeled my eyes away from his muscles and took inventory of my surroundings. Other than the broad-shouldered, politely-speaking, could-squash-me-with-his-pinky guy and me, the parking lot and surrounding areas were empty. I closed my car door, opening a clear escape path for my retreat then, pinching my keys between my fingers like a weapon – as if that would really help me against such a strong opponent – returned my attention to him.

The short tips of his hair were touched with the hints of summer. So, too, was his golden skin. "I have an appointment to look at a rental and I can't seem to figure out where it is." His eyes were focused on a scrap of paper he held in his hand.

I tried to sling my handbag over my shoulder nonchalantly, as if the sudden presence of a stranger – or the fact that he was uncomfortably close to penetrating my personal space – hadn't rattled me. Nonchalance failed me. Instead of looking calm and confident, I over-swung the bag and tipped my equilibrium. "What unit is it?" I pretended to be in control as I stabled myself against my car.

A set of cobalt blue eyes looked down at me. "Building F, unit twenty-four." He showed me the paper. Blue ink scratched out the simple address. "All I can seem to find is building E."

I took a deep breath and relaxed my guard enough to compose a sentence.

"F is right there," I said, pointing over my shoulder. Bad guys were brash and mean and ugly, right? They didn't take time for pleasantries before snatching up their prey. "Twenty-four is on the second floor. Probably that bi" – I stopped myself before blurting out the word bicep. Heat rose to my cheeks. "That balcony." Thoughtfully processing the words before letting them out of my mouth, I pointed to the balcony directly across from mine.

"Thanks." His soft eyes became even more exquisite when he smiled. "I'm Seth, by the way." He extended his hand to me. "And you are?"

I analyzed his movements, still not completely convinced that he wasn't some kind of threat, then slowly extended my hand towards his. "Ginger," I mumbled. The name still made me cringe.

"Well, Ginger." He wrapped his hand around mine and gave it a gentle pump. "I hope to see you around."

"Thank you." The words stumbled over my lips like a pre-pubescent girl who'd never talked to a good-looking guy before. I quickly redirected my gaze down to my tight pencil skirt and gently pushed my palms down the front of it. A few moments of silence followed then, without saying goodbye, I turned toward my condo and walked quickly away.

I thought I could feel his eyes following me as I made my way in small, controlled steps across the parking lot and up onto the sidewalk. I often felt this way – like I was being watched – but this time it was different. Something more than my typical paranoia.

Trying not to be too obvious, I twisted my head just enough to catch a glimpse of him out of the corner of my eye. As soon as my eyes contacted him, he seemed to look away. Like he had been looking at me, too. I told myself it wasn't creepy. But then, what was it? Either he was watching me or he was checking me out.

I shook both ideas immediately. I needed to turn my paranoia down a notch. Not one suspicious thing had happened to me in four months. And he most definitely wasn't checking me out. Guys like him never noticed geeky girls like me.

That's when I caught a glimpse of my reflection in the nearby apartment window. My blouse moved softly as the hot summer breeze pushed under the open collar and across my chest. Ginger's style – though it had been a tough adjustment for me – was definitely on the sexy side. A rush of excitement flew through my limbs. Maybe he *was* checking me out.

It was probably just a bout of wishful thinking, but that didn't stop my senses from reacting. My knees wobbled, trembling like a little fawn taking her first steps. Though I'd had four months practice in Ginger's impractical high-heeled shoes, I suddenly fought to maintain balance with each step I took. I'm sure I looked like Bambi, stumbling through his first steps. I slowed down my pace and counted my blessings that Kravitsch hadn't chosen that to be my name.

I slipped past the last of the hedges and turned into the stairwell alcove, rushing to get out of his line of sight. Gratefully, I didn't trip until I hit the third stair.

Closing the apartment door behind me, I shook off the strange twitterpation and childish nerves. It's not like I'd never seen a hot guy before. Or dated one. Okay, that was a stretch. Dating wasn't my thing. I didn't spend my free time fantasizing about a knight in shining armor or even a normal, average-Joe husband. I was an independent girl, perfectly content in my quiet, introverted, non-attached world. So much, in fact, I'd only dated a handful of guys. And not a single one of them had been as hot as "parking-lot-guy." Hotties like him don't go for geeks like me.

I latched the deadbolt then slid the security lock into place before checking the peephole to make sure he hadn't followed me.

Convinced that I was alone – and maybe a touch delusional – I set my handbag on the kitchen table, kicked my shoes off my feet, and opened my laptop. Aside from groceries, a personal laptop had been one of the first things I'd purchased after getting clearance to leave my purple prison that first week in Utah. I'd somewhat settled into my routine as a security analyst at the Utah based NSA Data Center – as much as one could when living a fake life, anyway. I clocked in each day, fulfilled my responsibilities to keep government and citizen data secure, then came home and tried to figure out how to put my life as Samantha back together.

While I waited for my machine to boot up, I walked over to the patio door and pulled the curtains open. I'd rarely opened the curtains let alone taken notice of the balcony across the way, but suddenly thoughts of my brief encounter in the parking lot had me wondering how long the unit had been empty. Admittedly, just like back home, I hadn't made any attempts to meet my neighbors. Which was fine. I didn't need the distraction that came with having friends. I had bigger things on my plate. Things like getting back to my life in Maryland and shedding the ridiculous cover I'd been stuck with, neither of which would happen until the case that had hauled me to the desert was solved.

I left the curtains open and turned back toward my computer. After four months in Utah, the surrounding mountains hadn't completely lost their appeal, but perhaps Seth would rent the space and I'd get a new view to look at.

My screen lit up. Grabbing a drink from the kitchen, I turned on some soft classical tunes then dove into my research.

Technically what I was doing in my free time wasn't illegal. Unethical, perhaps, in the backwards way I'd had to go about doing it, but not against any laws. I'd procured access to a few virtual servers and gone through great measures to assure that my setup was secure, all so I could tap into the deep layers of the darknet without being detected. All three of my servers were hosted in the Ukraine and planted behind a plethora of proxies that dead-ended to a non-existent server in Malaysia – eight-thousand miles from me and my purple apartment in Utah.

The media had jumped all over the case, dubbing the breach as PumpPurge, but I still referred to the gas hack as 43M. And I was convinced it was the reason I'd been so abruptly relocated. I must have been close to something or they wouldn't have perceived me as a threat and my life wouldn't have been so rudely uprooted. So, despite Kravitsch pulling me off the case and his further admonition to leave it alone, I kept digging. I needed to. I hungered for resolution and dedicated every minute of my personal time to finding it. There had to be a hole in the blackhat's code. Discovering it was the key to reclaiming my life.

A couple of hours passed before I peeled my eyes from the computer screen and got up to get some food. I gulped down a full glass of water then refilled the cup and, grabbing a yogurt from the fridge, walked back to the kitchen table. Sliding into my chair, I glanced out the patio door. A short, indulgent daydream about Seth began to form in my mind. It died almost as quickly as it had been born. The very notion was preposterous. I reclassified Seth as "parking-lot-guy" and filed him in my mind under the category of "never-going-to-happen."

I jotted a few notes onto the legal pad I kept beside my computer. Like the rest of my apartment, the notebook was clean. The cover looked as new as it had the day I bought it and each page was obsessively neat. I used only black gel-inked pens, the kind that slid smoothly across the page and made crisp, bold lines. I liked the order – needed it, even.

I reviewed my notes from the past few weeks then stared at the ceiling for several minutes. I needed to contact someone with an inside view of 43M. All the information in the world couldn't help me unless I could get it into the hands of someone who could do something about it. I needed an ally – or at least a sounding board.

I filed through my mental catalog of my current teammates, but came up short. I had purposefully set myself outside their circle. I wished I could go straight to Kravitsch. His inside knowledge and connections were exactly what I needed. But he'd intentionally taken me off the case. Going to him could be career suicide.

Suddenly, my balding, equally introverted, former coworker, David came to mind. He was a clock-in, clock-out, get-the-job-done-without-talking-to-anyone kind of guy. He was quick and bright, and fantastically quiet. And, if I'd understood Kravitsch correctly, the new owner of the 43M investigation. All of which made him exactly what I was looking for.

I dug through the internet until I found his name and contact information, then sent off a secure email to his personal account. Though he had no reason to trust a stranger, I hoped he wouldn't dismiss my email as a threat. I needed him to open it and, at the very least, look into my findings.

Early analysis had us initially believing that 43M was an external threat. We'd even tried to trace the malware to a teenaged developer in Ukraine. If David hadn't already, he'd soon learn that was a dead end. We'd spent months and months on the wrong track, chasing a fake trail. But, after hundreds of hours of unsanctioned research on my personal time, I'd finally made a breakthrough. The hack initiated from an abandoned amusement park in Bowling Green, Ohio. From there I'd found nothing but dead ends, but maybe, if he would open my email, David would find something that I couldn't. Maybe a fresh set of eyes would be the key to solving the case.

Closing out the browser tab with my email, I buried my efforts back into the numbers, patterns, and codes on my screen. A few more hours disappeared before I logged off and slid into my running shoes.

\*     \*     \*

The next day, as I stepped out of the NSA office building, the dry summer heat slapped me in the face with the same vengeance that it had each evening since mid-June. I twisted my sassy brunette curls into a messy knot on the top of my head then cranked the A/C up in my car for my six-minute commute. My hair wiggled free before making it home. I swept the parking lot with my eyes, then made a quick dash to the cool comfort of my condo.

I shed the light blue blouse and tight black trousers that Ninja-lady had provided me and slid into a pair of yoga pants and an MIT t-shirt that I'd procured online. It was an exact replica of one I picked up my senior year of college, and a comforting symbol of my old life. The only symbol I had, really. Not even my hair—which was still dyed dark—had grown back to its previous length. I had, however, grown fond of the sassy curls. Except when it was a million degrees outside. Then it was just plain hot. I ran my fingers through the loose locks and, grateful they were finally long enough to do so, pulled them back into a tight ponytail and opened up my laptop.

Just as I logged on, a knock sounded at my door.

I glanced at my screen, then over my shoulder at the door. I never had visitors.

The tapping sounded again, this time a little louder.

I closed my laptop and slid it under a couch cushion before hesitantly making my way to the door. Running my hand over both the security latch and the deadbolt, I assured they were locked, then pressed my eye to the peep-hole.

Parking-lot guy stood in near perfection on the stoop. I reminded myself his name was Seth, though I'd never really forgotten. I peered through the hole, past his azure eyes and broad shoulders, and into the hidden corners of the porch and stairs. He appeared to be alone. I backed away from the door so I could process my thoughts without being distracted by his looks. What could he possibly want? My mind and my body waged a battle with each other. Maybe he was dangerous, or maybe he was just a hot guy. Either way, he was a distraction… and a distraction was the last thing I wanted.

If I ignored him long enough, he'd go away.

He knocked again.

My hand, acting on its own will, unlatched the deadbolt.

"Hi." He grinned as I wedged the door open just enough to peek out. "I got the apartment," he boasted with a grin. "So" – his chest puffed up – "I guess that means we're going to be neighbors."

Still trying to figure out what had compelled me to open the door, I nearly tripped over two of the most basic words in the English language: "That's great."

Seth raised one of his brows. "Would you like to celebrate with me? I mean" – he took a step back. "Wow, that sounded super forward and creepy, didn't it? What I meant is . . ." He shook his head. "Ginger, right?" His lips twisted into a friendly grin.

I couldn't figure out why he was talking to me. Maybe my low-cut blouse had distracted him from noticing my whole geek vibe at our first meeting. A nod was all I could muster.

"Well, Ginger, have you eaten yet?"

Skeptical about his friendliness and equally self-conscious about my outfit, I tried to stay hidden behind the door. Hopefully I didn't sound as pathetic as I felt. "No," I answered. "I was just about to make something."

I didn't clarify that by *make something* I meant pour myself a bowl of Cocoa Puffs.

"Well, then, can I buy you dinner?" He seemed unfazed by my awkwardness. Maybe miracles did happen. Or maybe his battalion of thugs was hiding around the corner.

I processed the offer, still confused by his apparent interest in me. It's not that I wasn't somewhat attractive, but I certainly wasn't a beauty queen. Not that stuff like that really mattered, it's just . . .

"Come on." His voice broke into my thoughts. "Unless you've got something better to do."

I couldn't think of anything better than spending time with a hottie, except, of course, staying alive. "I'm kind of busy." I shrugged. Stupid paranoia.

"Are you sure?" He leaned against the handrail and casually tucked his thumbs into his front pockets. He wore a lighter pair of jeans today. They were slightly faded down the front but still immaculately clean and crisp.

No, I wasn't sure. I wanted to believe a hot guy like him could be genuinely interested in a girl like me but, let's face it, my geekdom had always been a tough sale. "Maybe another time," I offered. I doubted he'd try again.

"All right." He raised his hands in surrender. "But," he grinned again quickly, "you should know I don't give up easily."

If I'd known the first thing about witty retorts, I'd have thrown one out. Humor, however, was not a gift I possessed. I simply smiled.

Giving me a friendly nod, he started down the stairs.

"Seth," I called after him.

"Yes?" He turned around expectantly.

"I didn't catch your last name."

"Oh." His nose scrunched and his brows knitted together, making me feel mildly awkward about my need to analyze every little breeze that blew into my life. His nonchalant answer, however, helped put me at ease. "It's Smith," he said with a smile. "Seth Smith."

As soon as he disappeared down the stairs, I sat back down at my computer and began a new search.

# Chapter Four

Three days later a set of patio furniture arrived on the deck across from mine. That evening when I logged onto my computer, the mystery of Seth Smith distracted me yet again from my 43M research.

My new neighbor, as it turned out, shared his name with a professional baseball player, an online blogger, a geophysicist, and a plethora of other random men. The commonality of his name made it difficult to isolate information about him. However, digging is what I do best, so as I watched him step out his patio door and sink into his Adirondack chair, I reconvened my search.

Though he had a few social networking profiles, Seth, unlike my basement neighbor Tiffanie, didn't appear to be a social media junkie. His infrequent and non-descript posts made hacking into his life a bit of a challenge. Of course, if he ran the same test on me, he'd have come up empty.

I bobbed between the "Who is Seth?" spreadsheet I'd created and the man lounging on the patio across from mine. The summer sun danced off his tanned skin, and a light breeze played with the tips of his dark blond hair. The more I tried to focus on my computer screen, the more I realized I was staring at him.

Coupling the skiff of information I'd been able to gather from Seth's social networking posts with my network knowledge base, I did a quick search through public government records. When that didn't pan out much information, I hacked into a few "dark" databases for more details. He had a New Jersey birth certificate and driver's license, a clean criminal record, and a bank account at Provident Bank. He seemed legit enough— not exactly the type of guy who'd work with a blackhat to destroy my apartment or threaten my life.

I logged into my email, hoping for a response from David. Nothing. Nada. Not even a cursory thanks. I don't know why I was disappointed. It's not like I'd expected a response anyway. Shrugging it off, I closed out my email and minimized my Seth spreadsheet, then dove into 43M.

The sun was casting a long shadow across my balcony when I decided to log out for the night. It was earlier than I typically shut my research down but, even though Seth no longer lounged on his patio, I was too distracted to be productive. I decided an early run was in order.

Plugging an earbud into my ear, I stretched my hamstrings on the bottom stair then started a slow run down the sidewalk. As I rounded the corner of my building, my momentum came to a rigid halt.

"Sorry." A set of hands grabbed my shoulders to stabilize me from doing a face plant. "I didn't see you coming."

I flinched backwards and, throwing my hands protectively in front of me, righted myself. I was embarrassed about the collision but not ready to drop my guard.

"No problem," I finally said after realizing the person behind the hands had no apparent intention to attack me. "I'm the klutz, not you."

"Just bad timing." Seth slid his hands off my shoulders, then offered a dismissive wave. His tank top stretched tightly over the muscles in his chest and torso. His deltoids formed tight triangles at the base of his neck. Veins bulged out of his biceps and up into his shoulders.

My chest pounded, though I'd barely begun my run. I tugged on the hem of my tank top, unsure how to manage the unexpected interaction. "I" – I floundered for a response.

He filled the silence for me. "Are you coming or going?" he asked with a kindness that made me wonder why I had to be so jumpy.

"Going," I answered, though if my intent was solitude, I should've lied. His attire – the tank top, athletic shorts, and running shoes – served as a pretty good indication that he, too, was planning a workout.

"Do you mind if I join you?"

I tried not to obsess about the way he seemed to have appeared from nowhere. Or that he'd conveniently chosen to run at the same pre-dusk hour as I did. Or, for that matter, that he made my stomach fill with butterflies even though he was still just as much out of my league as he'd been three days before.

Reminding myself that I'd checked into his background, I pushed aside my paranoia. "Sure." I shrugged, not totally comfortable with the idea of sharing my personal time with a stranger, but for some reason unable to tell him no.

"Great," he smiled. "You lead."

I resituated my earbuds and turned my music on then set our pace and path.

We'd run the perimeter of the condo complex and were entering the streets of a residential development before he attempted conversation. "So, Ginger." The name didn't sound quite so ridiculous as it rolled off his tongue. "Tell me about yourself."

Talking while running wasn't something I was used to. Neither, for that matter, was small talk in any form. The combination alone made me feel awkward. The fact that my whole life was fiction made it even worse.

"Nothing to tell," I shrugged.

"Come on," he pushed. "Unless you just hatched from an egg yesterday, you've got to have something to tell."

"I'm just your run-of-the-mill, boring kind of girl." I considered powering off my music but, hoping to avoid conversation, decided to leave it on play.

"I don't believe that for a second."

Seth ran comfortably by my side, seemingly unfazed by our pace, though I was starting to feel it. Despite the burning in my legs and chest, I upped my speed and – hoping the quickened pace didn't kill me – waited for him to drill me for more information. He never did.

We ran a loop through the exterior streets of the subdivision, finishing a six-mile stint before slowing our pace to a walk.

"I'm impressed," Seth said as he wiped his arm across his glistening forehead. "I didn't expect you to be able to keep up that pace for so long."

Me either. My lungs felt like they were being ripped out of my chest. "I run a lot," I answered through labored breath. Who was this guy? And how had he issued a compliment and an invitation for small talk, all in one little sentence?

"That's cool." He positioned his hands on his hips and drew in a deep breath of his own. Sweat cascaded over his jawline and down his neck, pooling in a V across the front of his shirt. "I still haven't quite adjusted to the altitude here."

"It takes some time." My labored breath indicated that I hadn't fully adjusted either.

"Are you one of those marathon chicks?"

I considered the question for an uncomfortable minute. "No," I finally offered then, sure he wasn't going to settle for a simple yes or no answer, added, "It's just a hobby I picked up from my dad." Living in a world of lies, it was nice to share a truth, even if it was a small one. What I didn't tell him – and never would – was that once upon a time I was a chunky, little band geek. I'd taken up running in high school not only as a way to connect with my dad, but because if anyone's self-esteem needed the endorphins, it was mine.

"Ah." He nodded. "That's cool."

He walked with me to the base of my building's stairs. I immediately started up them, hoping he'd take this as a cue that I wasn't really up for a conversation.

"Thanks for running with me," he called behind me.

"Anytime," I called over my shoulder before slipping through my front door. I bit my lip as I pushed the door closed and secured all the locks. *Anytime?* What was I thinking. I had bigger things to do than flirt around with some random guy. Even if he was ridiculously hot and made my insides turn to goo. And most especially since he had the same effect on my brain.

# CHAPTER FIVE

F ive days and still no response from David. I
wondered if knowing my true identity would
make any difference. We hadn't exactly been
friends, but as far as introverts go, we had at least been
friendly.

Maybe I was naïve to think I could trust him. But
if not David, then who? I drafted another email then
deleted it. Desperate as I was for answers, I still needed
to take precautions. Since sending my previous email, I'd
dug up some strangely familiar looking code in the 43M
trail. Like artists, many coders had their own little
trademarks, even if they didn't recognize them
themselves. The familiarity of the script baffled me –

mostly because I couldn't put a finger on where I'd seen it before.

I decided to try to discover who the author was before I tried to contact David again.

Several hours passed before I pulled my eyes from the screen. As much as I loved the hunt, hours upon hours and days upon days of research had started to bog me down. I was slowly losing hope of ever finding answers.

I waited a little later to go for a run than I had the previous night, hoping that it would deter Seth from accompanying me. As soon as I walked out my front door, I realized how wrong I was.

"Ah," he smiled from his perch on the bottom stair. "I was beginning to wonder if you weren't really the runner you claimed to be."

"How long have you been sitting there?" Always on guard, I scanned my eyes down the sides of his torso and over the curve at the base of his back looking for any sign of a weapon.

Shrugging his shoulders, he stood. "I don't know. Maybe an hour or so."

"For reals?" I shook my head and noted that the only thing hidden under his running clothes were the cuts and bulges of firm muscles.

He puffed his chest, as if he thought I was checking him out, and nodded.

"You sat here for an hour just waiting for me to show up?" *What was wrong with this guy? Or, better yet, what was wrong with me?*

"Yep." He grinned. "Lucky for me, you showed up just in time. I was about to give up on you."

"Next time I'll know to hold out a little longer," I said. Sadly, I was only half-joking.

\*       \*       \*

Despite my calculated efforts to switch up my running times over the next couple of days, Seth showed up in similar fashion the following two evenings. And, each time I saw him, I played nice but secretly wished he'd go away. Not that I hadn't enjoyed his company but ... I didn't even know what my 'but' was anymore. He'd been nothing but polite and non-intrusive on our previous runs. He hadn't asked a lot of questions and he'd been respectful of my personal space. Plus, I felt safer when he was near. Like I had my own personal body guard.

"Did you grow up around here?" he asked as we came close to the end of our six-mile loop. It was our fourth run together and somehow we'd continually managed to maintain the rapid pace I'd set the first night he'd bumped into me. He ran a hand through his damp hair. It stood straight up for a moment then fell back into its perfectly groomed, messy spikes.

*If you consider 2000 miles close, then yes.* I stopped and bent over, resting the palms of my hands on my thighs as I drew several deep breaths. "I was an Army brat," I thoughtfully answered. "I grew up all over the place." It was only a partial lie—a slightly modified version of the one I'd told my coworkers. Though my family had lived all over the world, the better half of my adolescence we'd been stationed in Virginia. When my dad retired, he'd opened an auto shop there.

"Really?" He stopped just in front of me then, turning around to face me, raised his brows. "That's pretty cool. I'll bet you've been to some great places."

I drew another deep breath then, settling my hands on my hips, straightened my stance and resumed walking. "Yes, I have." Another truth. I was on a roll. "How about you?" I asked, emboldened by my desire to confirm the data I'd collected on him. "Where are you from?"

"Jersey." He fell back in beside me.

I made a mental check then prodded deeper, "You don't sound like you're from Jersey." It was the one fact in his personal data that had seemed off to me. I'd met my share of Jersey natives and all of them had an undeniable accent. He didn't have the slightest hint of a Jersey drawl.

"Well, I suppose that's just one of the casualties of my job."

*Casualties of the job?* He had no idea. The look on my face must have asked the question on my mind.

"I work for a consulting firm," he offered without my asking. "Boring, blah kind of stuff."

I made another notch on my mental check-list. He was two for two with the information I'd gathered.

"How about you, Ginger? What do you do?"

Back to me and my fictitious life again. I carried a lot of secrets, and even before I'd been deposited in the Utah desert, this had been one of them. Anonymity was part of the NSA code. "I work for the Department of Defense." I recited my trained answer.

"Really? I've got a buddy that works there. Which department are you in?"

I'd been sworn not to draw attention to the NSA, but I was authorized to disclose a blanketed version of my affiliation if asked. "The NSA," I finally offered.

"So, you're a spy?" His entire face lit up.

"No." I shook my head. It was a common misconception fed by the media. I'd heard it a million times. "Just computer stuff. Data analytics. Pretty boring, really." Until the day your apartment blows up and they ship you clear across the country.

"Boring?" He stopped walking and looked at me. "Are you kidding? I'll bet you deal with some pretty intense stuff."

NSA policy was simple—nothing in, nothing out—including details. "Not really." I kept walking.

He fell back to my side as if he hadn't missed a step. "You'd probably have to kill me if you told me, right?" He laughed.

I hadn't realized how closely he'd settled beside me until he playfully bumped my shoulder with his. I took a half a step sideways.

"Not me personally." I smirked. "But I'd imagine there's someone on the payroll who takes care of that." It was intended as a joke until I remembered Andre, the security agent who'd escorted me out of Maryland. He seemed like he might be able to pull off something like that.

We stopped at the bottom of the stairs by my condo.

"Well," he chuckled, "I hope you're not ready to call a hit on me just yet." He leaned against the stair rail and focused his eyes on me.

I calculated the probability of actually getting involved with Seth then ran a quick risk assessment based off our limited interaction and the information I'd gathered. I balanced out the "this doesn't make sense" with the "I'll never know if I don't try" before a string of fumbled words slid past my lips.

"Look," I said. "I appreciate you running with me these last few days, I really do. But, honestly, I'm not looking for any new friends right now."

"Okay." He lifted his chin and locked his eyes on mine. "So, instead of running tomorrow, can I buy you dinner?"

"Umm, did you hear what I just said?"

He smiled. "Yes. I heard you. And I think I know what you're saying, but I'd still like to take you to dinner."

"Cocky much?"

"I prefer confident. But really, in my defense, I told you straight up that I was persistent. I asked you to dinner a week ago and I refuse to give up until you take me up on the offer."

"So, if I go, you'll leave me alone?" I bit the sides of my cheeks, trying to hold back the smile that kept trying to form. I was trying to dodge him but he seemed to think I was flirting.

"I'll try."

"It's really a yes or no question."

"Hmm."

"Do or do not, there is no try." I quoted one of my favorite lines from one of my favorite movies.

"Ah, Yoda. So much wisdom in that one." He took a step back and, with a wink, said, "I'll pick you up at seven."

"I didn't say yes."

"You didn't say no."

\*       \*       \*

I didn't say no. And I spent the next day at work trying to figure out why. I was on a mission and it did not involve hooking up with the first hot guy that looked my way. Granted, in my defense, he was *the* very first – and only – hot guy who'd ever actually looked my way. But that was no justification for letting him distract me from getting my life back.

I processed and processed – and then processed again – trying to figure out what was going on with me. Nothing made sense. I didn't want to hang out with Seth – or really anyone for that matter – but stupid-girl showed up in my head every time he appeared and I didn't know how to combat her . . . or him, for that matter. I tried to dissect the situation from a scientific approach, but all the algorithms and probabilities in the world couldn't help me figure out what he saw in me. Or why he kept coming around despite the cold shoulder I'd tried so hard to give him.

And they definitely couldn't explain why my heart raced at the very thought of him.

When he showed up at my door to pick me up, I was secretly glad that I hadn't thought of a legit reason to tell him no. Kind of.

"Do you mind if I change first?" I glanced down at my business slacks and plain white blouse. I'd grown accustomed to wearing a few buttons down and letting my collar lay more open like the little Ninja-lady had shown me. Suddenly, though, I mentally cinched up the collar, conscious that the slight hint of cleavage might give him the wrong impression about my intentions. I was hoping to make tonight our last encounter so I could refocus my energy on my mission.

"Of course not," he said, casual and cool as ever. "Take your time."

"Thanks," I said. "It's been a busy day and I haven't had a chance to change." I pushed the door closed and turned toward the hallway before realizing how rude my behavior was. The guy was taking me to dinner. The least I could do was invite him in.

I looked around the place. Boring and beige, except for the screaming purple wall. Not really a good representation of me, but neither was my brown hair, colored contacts, or flaunting breasts.

I shook my head as I opened the door. "Sorry. It's really hot out there. Please, come in."

He smiled and followed me into my condo, bringing the woodsy smell of his cologne with him. I picked my laptop up from its home on the kitchen table and, taking it with me, slipped into my bedroom to change. I tried on seven different brightly hued shirts before finally settling on one that wasn't too loud to be me, but not too dull to be Ginger. Taking one last peak in the mirror, I zipped up my jeans and vowed to get rid of Mr. Hot-distraction before the end of the night.

When I came back out, Seth was leaning against my kitchen counter, the muscles on his arms and chest stretching his shirt like an airbrushed GQ model. The purple wall paled in contrast to his smile.

"Ready?" he asked, turning his lips up into an even bigger grin. My heart quickened. Between his jewel-like eyes and the smoothness of his voice, his mere presence was intoxicating.

"Yes," I answered, trying not to sound as giddy as I suddenly felt. I was going on a date – I corrected myself, it was just dinner – with a man who didn't wear his cell phone on his belt. A man who didn't have wide-rimmed glasses or a collection of super-hero t-shirts. A man with good hygiene and actual, real-life social skills.

I picked my handbag up from its typical resting spot on the kitchen table and reached inside. I didn't keep much in it: a tube of lip balm, a pack of gum, my work badge, my car keys, and my cell phone. All was in order, except my phone. It wasn't there. Glancing at the coffee table, I patted down my jean pockets.

"I just need to grab my phone," I said as I mentally retraced my steps. "I don't remember pulling it out of my bag." I looked at the empty spot on the kitchen table where I'd been sitting with my laptop. My notebook was there, its simple black cover folded cleanly over months and months of 43M notes. Two black gel pens lay parallel across its top. "Maybe I took it back to my room."

I tossed my purse over my shoulder and did another visual sweep of my apartment as I walked back to my bedroom. It wasn't with my laptop on my dresser, or in the pile of discarded shirts, or even on the bathroom counter.

"Is this it?" Seth called from the kitchen.

I rushed out of my bedroom as he lifted the phone off the counter and held it up for me to see.

I breathed a sigh of relief. "Yes," I answered as heat rushed to my cheeks. "Where was it?"

He laughed. "It was right over here." He pointed. "By the kitchen sink."

I must have looked like a silly, scatter-brained fool. If not, I certainly felt like one. I took the phone – my only connection to the people running my life – and tucked it into my pocket. Losing things wasn't part of my modus operandi. Neither, for that matter, was having the Greek god Adonis in my kitchen.

# Chapter Six

Somehow I managed to make it down the stairs and into the parking lot without tripping over my feet or my tongue. I could count the number of actual, for-real dates I'd had on one hand. I didn't intend for this to be one of them. As he clicked the fob on his keychain, however, I got the hint that Seth did.

The lights on his silver BMW flashed as the doors unlocked. I'd never been quite the car-junkie my mechanic dad had hoped I'd be, but the fine, crisp lines of a BMW had a mesmerizing effect on pretty much anyone with a heartbeat. "Nice," I whispered under my breath as I approached the passenger door. Still admiring the car, I reached for the handle, but Seth had managed to slide around me. His hand lightly brushed mine away as he pulled the door open for me.

"I was taught that a gentleman should always get the door for a lady."

"Thank you." I swooned. A gentleman? I'd never dated – not dated – one of those before. He waited for me to settle into the soft, leather seat, before closing the door.

Every inch of the car was immaculately detailed, from the perfectly vacuumed floors to the spotless windshield. He started the car then pushed a button that made the hard-top lift away from the windshield. Three pieces folded over each other while the trunk compartment lifted open. In one, fluid motion, the stacked pieces of the top slid into the compartment and the lid closed.

"You don't mind, do you?" Seth pointed to the open sky above us.

"No." My own car – the one I'd left in the employee garage in Maryland – was a convertible Mini Cooper. Not quite the same scale of awesome as his Beemer, but it fit me nicely. "I actually enjoy driving topless."

He raised his brow ever so slightly and tipped his head toward me with a grin. "You don't say?" He was trying not to laugh.

I may have made it down the stairs without a fumble, but apparently that was as far as my social filters were going to take me. "I mean the car," I quickly corrected. Heat rushed into my cheeks and I had to look away. This was exactly why I didn't socialize with people.

"If you say so." I could hear the grin in his voice.

Afraid of what other faux pas might slip past my lips, I zipped my mouth and looked out the passenger side of the car.

As soon as we turned out of the apartment complex, Seth hit the throttle. Wind whipped around the windshield and twisted through my hair. I reached up and, roping as much of the brunette tornado as I could, pulled it into a knot at the base of my neck.

"Too much?" He yelled over the wind and the stereo.

I shook my head no. He settled two fingers at the base of the steering wheel and relaxed back into his seat.

"What kind of music do you like?" He pointed at the stereo with his free hand.

I shrugged. "I don't care." I was getting pretty good with the lies, but this one was justified. Most people laughed when they found out my playlist was filled with a combination of techno and classical music.

"Come on." He flipped through the stations. "Rock?"

I shrugged.

He pushed the button again. "Pop?"

I shrugged again.

"So," he filtered through a couple stations then settled on one. "Country?"

"Sure," I said, not because I agreed, but because I sensed that he wasn't going to stop until I appeased his curiosity.

"I think you're lying."

He had no idea how right he was. "Why would you think that?" I defended.

"Who sings this song?" He turned the music up a notch.

I listened to the lyrics, totally unaware who the voice behind them was. The singer was definitely male and the ballad about how sexy his tractor was, was definitely country.

"Come on," he baited. "Every country fan knows this one. It's an oldy."

Everything I knew about country music boiled down to one CD my dad owned. There was a black hatted cowboy on the cover – I chuckled to myself at the modern connection to cyber hacking. No wonder I remembered the CD. Black hat was a term used for a hacker with malicious intent. I chuckled again then refocused my memory.

In addition to his large, black hat, the man on the cover wore a black and blue striped shirt. His thumbs were tucked under the top of his over-sized belt loop. "Garth Brooks," I remembered out loud.

"I commend your effort, but no. This is Kenny Chesney." He sang a few more of the lyrics, then flipped the station again.

The scanner stopped on a classical station. Vivaldi's *The Four Seasons* played out over the speakers. I turned my face toward the passenger side of the car again and, closing my eyes, let the soft tones move over me.

"Is this it?" he asked again.

I responded with my same shrug. If I admitted to loving it, would he raise me another notch on his geek meter?

He didn't ask again and he didn't change the station.

The summer sun still hung high over the eastern horizon as he maneuvered his car through the light suburb traffic. The open top made conversation difficult but that didn't stop him from throwing out questions every time we came to a stop.

"Where did you go to school? What was your major? Do you have a favorite TV show? . . . Really, you don't watch TV?"

This was exactly why I hated dating. Or hanging out in general. Even before I was Ginger, I'd found it easier not to socialize. And definitely less stress to not to have friends. Not that I'd have ever admitted it to anyone, but the simple truth was that I just didn't want to get hurt. If I didn't open myself up – if I didn't give my heart away – then there was no chance of getting it broken. It was a mistake I'd made once before. And one I didn't anticipate making again.

\*       \*       \*

The aroma of chow mien and Kung Pow chicken filled the little strip mall restaurant, tickling my taste buds before we even ordered. It had been months since I'd ventured out to a restaurant and anything would have been great, but when Seth declared that Chinese food was his favorite, I couldn't help but smile. It was hard to believe that his favorite cuisine was the exact same as mine. Then again, and despite my best efforts to find a flaw and send him packing, he seemed so perfect that pretty much everything about him was hard to believe.

"Cats or dogs?" He asked as we waited for the waitress to bring us our food.

"Um," I shrugged. "I don't know."

"Come on," he smiled. "You've got to have an opinion. I don't believe you're the boring, vanilla kind of girl you've been pretending to be. Everyone's got opinions."

I did. Lots of them. I just didn't believe in sharing them.

His blue eyes penetrated mine. They were almost the same shade as my natural color. Softer, though. More enticing. The pressure was almost too much. "Dogs," I finally answered.

"See," he smiled. "That wasn't so hard. Let's try another one: mornings or nights?"

I twisted my hands on my lap. These were stupid questions but that didn't stop my heart from racing or my palms from sweating. "Nights."

"Now we're on a roll." He clasped his hands together and fired off another simple question. Then another.

I satisfied him with single word answers.

Thoughts of 43M kept trying to push their way to the front of my mind. I knew I needed to be digging even deeper into the darknet and expanding my research to corners I'd never been before. I was so close to a resolution, I could feel it.

But, there was something about Seth that made me feel okay about taking a breather. Almost. As if taking a break from my data digging obsession wouldn't have dire consequences. Who was I kidding? A few short hours of reprieve wouldn't kill me.

I gave my hands a final twist under the table then, reaching for my drink, made a conscious decision to make the most of my night out. Maybe taking a break every now and then would be good for me. Maybe I'd gotten so close to the solution that I couldn't see it. Maybe it was sitting right under my nose.

The waitress delivered our meals and I, cautious not to make a mess or a scene in any way, picked up my chopsticks and slowly dug in. Seth's questions slowed down as he did the same, but they didn't stop.

He shook his head. "You know, Ginger, you're so talkative I'm having a hard time getting a word in edgewise here."

I looked up at him. Sarcasm. I spoke it with some degree of capability – inside my head. Verbalizing it, though, was something my mind and mouth couldn't seem to work out. I simply said, "Sorry."

"Nah, there's nothing to be sorry about. I'm sorry if I made you feel that way. There's nothing wrong with being quiet. I get it. You're a private kind of girl. No harm in that. It just makes me wonder . . .?" He trailed off for a moment. "Makes me wonder what you're thinking about. What you're holding back." He paused for another few, eternally long seconds. "Or what you're holding on to. Do you have a boyfriend?"

Why in the world would he wonder that? I shook my head.

"Maybe an old flame that's still burning?"

I shook my head again. I may have gone against all rational reasoning and opened my heart to Peter, and it may have shattered into a million pieces when we decided, somewhat mutually, that we were better off without each other. But I wasn't just kind-of over him, I was completely over him. No flame. Not even a single ember.

"Hmm." He waggled his chopsticks above his plate. "You're a tough one to figure out, but I'm going to do it."

Part of me wanted to encourage him and the other part wanted to warn him that it was a hopeless venture. I simply smiled then shifted my eyes back toward my plate.

I took a few more bites, wondering with each one, what his next question would be.

"So, you're a data analyst, right?"

"Yes." One word.

"That's computer stuff, correct?"

"Yes."

"So, you're on a computer all day?"

I nodded.

"And then you come home and get on it again?"

I shifted my eyes toward him. How did he know what I did when I got home?

He balanced a scoop of rice on his chopsticks like a pro. "I see you on your computer almost every night. Well, not exactly. I see the glow from it, not the actual computer. But I figure it's a computer because I'd probably be able to see your TV screen. And you said you didn't watch TV, so what else could it be?"

I shrugged.

"You seem to stay up pretty late with it. Not that I'm spying on you or anything." His defense was playful. "It's just hard to miss the blue glow coming from an otherwise dark apartment."

I shrugged again, embarrassed that he'd noticed, but at the same time taking note that he'd clearly been watching me. I wondered what he was up to before admitting that, until he'd arrived, I'd never opened my curtains. If I didn't want to be seen, I should've kept them drawn. It was only logical to think that a neighbor – or anyone who'd wanted to spy on me – might have a view of my space. So much for keeping my head on a swivel.

"Sorry." He tilted his head as he smiled at me. "That was kind of invasive, wasn't it?" He lifted his hands as if in surrender. "I didn't mean it to be."

I looked down at my plate, considering a response while I pushed a piece of chicken around with my wooden chopsticks. I felt vulnerable, and not just to him. I hadn't realized how lax I'd gotten at keeping myself and my movements secret.

Still trying to decide the best way to answer, I picked a piece of chicken up and popped it in my mouth. I couldn't tell him about 43M and most definitely couldn't let on that I spent my nights undergrounding as a hacker.

"You know" – he grinned – "it's not my business what you do late at night. In the dark. Alone." His wink made it feel like an accusation, like he thought I was doing something naughty. Okay, in a sense I was, but not what he seemed to be implying.

I tried not to choke on the battered poultry — or his words. So much for him trying to be a gentleman. "I play games," I finally offered after I'd finished my coughing fit. It seemed like a believable defense.

"What kind of games?" he winked again, seemingly pleased with the suggestion behind his words.

Heat rose to my cheeks. Did he know what he was doing? Had he intended his words to make me feel awkward? Was he flirting? Why did I not know how to flirt?

"I used to have a buddy that was hooked on *World of Warcraft*," he continued nonchalantly as if his previous words hadn't been bawdy. "What do you play?"

I took another bite of my chicken, chewed it slowly, then answered. "I used to play *WOW*." It wasn't a lie, though I hadn't played since high school. "Now I mostly play RPG's like *Dragon Age: Inquisition*."

Seth twisted his fingers around his chopsticks, looking at me as if he were genuinely interested in my geekisms. "I've never heard of that one. Maybe I should download it and we can play together sometime."

I set my chopsticks down and wrapped my hand around my drink, hoping he wasn't serious. My total experience with the game was what I'd overheard my coworkers say about it. Two minutes in and he'd know I'd lied. I pressed my glass to my lips and took a long sip.

"You know," I said as I pulled my drink away from my lips, "for some reason I hadn't really pegged you as a gamer."

His lips curled up into a smile. "Nor me, you."

I was afraid to ask what he'd have pegged me as instead. "I guess we all have secrets," I said. It was the understatement of the year.

"Not me." He raised his eyebrows. "I'm an open book."

"And obviously a liar." I raised a brow back at him. Nobody was truly an open book.

"What do you want to know?" He set his chopsticks down and raised his chin.

"You tell me," I smirked.

He clasped his hands in front of his chest and twisted his lips as if he were giving it deep thought. "I don't like chocolate."

"Shut up! That's not even a thing. Everybody likes chocolate."

"Not me." His expression remained solid.

I pointed at him with my chopsticks, unwilling to believe his words. "How do you even survive in this world without chocolate?"

He relaxed his hands and leaned back in his chair. "I like to consider myself somewhat of an anomaly."

"You think?"

"You know," he said with a smile, "it's not a bad thing to be different. Sometimes different is a good thing."

"Have you even tried chocolate?" I just couldn't shake the idea from my mind. It was a travesty.

He nodded his head.

"Like, different kinds of chocolate? You know, they're not all created equal, right?"

His shoulders raised in a half-shrug. "I'm a man who has learned not to form opinions too quickly. I don't judge people on first impressions. I don't take my clients at face value. I don't sign contracts without doing my homework. And, I most definitely didn't form my opinion against chocolate based on a single experience."

Through the rest of the evening, those few sentences were the ones that stuck with me. He didn't judge people on first impressions and he didn't take his clients at face value. For a half a second I wondered if that's what I was: a client. But then I shook the idea. If he was out to get me – or even if he was trying to garner information from me – he was doing a terrible job.

Either he was a nice guy looking for friends or, for some inexplicable reason, he actually liked me. Neither scenario mattered. I had a task at hand, and he had no part in it.

# CHAPTER SEVEN

I obsessed over my research for the next couple of nights, skipping my nightly run and often even dinner. I had to close things up, and I needed to do it quickly. If I didn't find resolution soon, I was going to lose my mind.

Maybe I already had.

The line between secrets and lies was getting thin.

There were only two contacts in Ginger's phone: the mystery, over-seeing protector who'd become my source for instruction. I'd named him *The Keeper* in my phone's contacts. And Kravitsch.

I called the second one. "It's my mom's birthday," I said as soon as he answered.

"Hello Ginger."

"Samantha." I thumbed through the assortment of colorful cards on the greeting card aisle of my local grocery store. My gut had been churning all day. I was ready to break.

"Ginger."

"It's my mom's birthday," I repeated. "Do you have any idea what it's like to be two-thousand miles across the country from your mom and not be able to contact her to wish her a happy birthday?" I fidgeted with the card in my hand. It had a photo of a bulldog on the front and a crack inside about being the best kid in the world. My mom would've loved it. It was perfectly suited to her humor. "Does she even know that I'm alive?"

I'd waxed somber all day, breaking at the reality that I could have no contact with my mom on her special day. Or any day for that matter. It's not like I needed her to hold my hand or sing me to sleep each night, but a phone call or a greeting card, even if it was only on a quarterly basis, seemed like a reasonable thing to ask for.

"We've been through this already. I assure you that your parents know that you are okay." His voice was as dry as the Utah desert in July.

"You assure me?" I sighed. "Like you assure me that you've been working on getting me home?" I was trying not to be cynical, I really was, but if I'd been able to crack into 43M on my own, why hadn't the team he'd *assured* me was on it, been able to make headway?

"I am under no obligation to keep you up to date on that case," Kravitsch monotoned through the line. "But I think you will be interested to know that we've had a recent crack in the case that affects you and we're moving in a good direction."

*Like, as in, the direction of moving me home?* I held the snarky question to myself. "Thank you," I played nice. Did he know I'd sent information to David? I couldn't help but gloat at my belief that that's where their sudden crack had come from. "Are you sure there is nothing I can do to move this process along faster? I've got nothing but time on my hands, please put me to work."

"You can help by staying out of it."

I smashed the card back into its spot on the rack. "What if I don't?"

"Then you're not as smart as you think you are."

"Will you fire me?"

"Only if you break the law."

"I'm done, Kravitsch."

"Quitting isn't going to magically change the situation. You got caught up in someone's business. You really pissed them off. This isn't going to just disappear."

I held back the tears that wanted to push out of my soul.

"We'll get you home as soon as possible," he said. "Until then, for the safety of yourself and those around you, keep your nose where it ought not to be."

"Yes, sir," I answered, knowing full well that I wouldn't. This was *my* life, I certainly wasn't going to sit back and wait for someone else to fix it.

I finished up my grocery shopping, trying my best to ignore the knot in my chest as thoughts of the quiet, non-assuming life I'd left behind pushed into my head. The cool waters off the Virginia shoreline called to my heart and my mind. I missed the trees and the green and my car. I loved my car. If I could just go for a spin in my car, with the top down and the wind in my hair, maybe things wouldn't seem so bleak.

As I passed the bakery, I lost my composure. My jaw quivered and silent tears rolled down my cheeks. What kind of daughter didn't wish her mom a happy birthday?


I marched up the steps to my apartment, a can of paint in one hand and my groceries in the other, intent on unburying a piece of Samantha before I lost all grip on reality. I hadn't been real picky about a color – anything other than the plum nightmare that had greeted me each day would have been fine – so I'd just picked up a can of mis-mixed paint off the clearance shelf. The calm shade of gray was sure to be an upgrade.

Leaving all of my curtains closed, I put the last of my groceries away then headed to my bedroom to change my clothes. I slid into a pair of yoga pants then started to unbutton my blouse. Two buttons down I changed my mind. I hated the fitted purple blouse as much as I hated the loud purple wall. They could die together as far as I was concerned.

Stopping at the bathroom mirror to pull my hair up, I paused at the brown eyes staring back at me. There was nothing ginger about Ginger. Her brown eyes and brown hair were about as far from my natural look as I could have been. I couldn't do anything about restoring my red hair – I had to report to work as a brunette – but I could bask in the beauty of my blue eyes in the privacy of my own apartment.

Leaning in to the mirror, I pressed my finger to first one eye and then the other.

"There she is." I drew a refreshing breath as I secured the brown contacts in their case and pushed them to the side of the vanity. Two bright blue eyes smiled back at me. "I'm still here."

An hour later I'd covered the purple wall with its first coat of gray. Satisfied with my work, I made a peanut butter sandwich and, sitting on the counter, used my phone's browser to place an order for a poster of the Virginia coastline. To an outsider, it would simply look like a framed photo of a beach. To me, it represented home.

Paint curled off the end of my roller, dripping into a blob on the tile floor as I started the second coat. I'd already spotted my shirt with paint dots, so I took it off and used it to mop up the mess. Between the fresh coat of paint and the wadded up purple blouse on the floor, I felt a sense of freedom I hadn't felt since changing my identity. It was confirmation – if only to myself – that Samantha was alive and well.

I pressed my hands to my hips and, with genuine satisfaction, smiled at my new gray wall. Pleased that my chore was complete, I wrapped the roller in my shirt and tossed them both in the kitchen trash.

I hadn't realized how late it had gotten until a knock on the door pulled me out of my thoughts. Even the sight of Seth through my peephole wasn't enough to break my home-sick reflections. He rocked back and forth in his running shoes, adjusting the buds in his ears as he awaited my answer.

I looked down at myself, my polka-dot bra reminding me that I'd tossed my shirt in the trash and had nothing on top but a few strands of satin and lace. Seth and I had run together several times, and – if I was being honest with myself – the mere thought of him made me buzz. Maybe that's why I'd avoided him since our dinner date. Was it really even a date? I didn't know.

Regardless, I didn't think we were at a point in our relationship where greeting him in my underwear was appropriate. I wasn't even sure what kind of relationship we had. Were we friends? Running buddies? Or something more?

I pushed off the idea of being 'something more.' He was pretty much everything I'd ever dreamed of finding, and I was – I sighed. I was Ginger. A covert girl living in a covert world.

Pretend.

Fake.

I pressed my back to the door and slowly melted down it. Samantha would've loved Seth. Too bad they'd never meet each other.

*     *     *

I cried myself to sleep that night. The next morning, however, I was reset and ready to push past my frustration. Everybody had a right to have secrets. Me included. If I had to be Ginger, if I had to live in Utah, and if I *had* to spend some time with a man ridiculously out of my league, then I might as well embrace it. All of it.

By noon I resolved to do something that Samantha would have never done. So, determined to follow through, I pushed logic and reservation out the window and, at long last, took a step out of my comfort zone.

Pretending to be spontaneous wasn't easy, though. Some people were born with the innate ability to jump without thought. Those carefree traits, however, weren't something you could magically acquire overnight. In fact, it took me all day to devise a concrete plan that didn't look overly thought out or deliberate. My strategy involved a calculated effort to appear impulsive and carefree—two things I definitely knew little about.

"I hope you're hungry," I said with more confidence than I felt as Seth opened his apartment door. I'd purposefully dressed in one of Ginger's shortest skirts and flirty blouses. "There is no way I can eat this whole pie on my own." I'd practiced my invitation the entire drive home, hoping it would sound somewhat clever.

Propping the door just wide enough to fill the space with his body, he tucked one hand in his jeans pocket and leaned against the door frame, cool as ever. "Homemade," he teased. "My favorite." One cheek lifted higher than the other when he smiled.

"It's not chocolate." I'd challenged myself not to trip over my words or say anything nerdy for the next few hours.

"Well, that's a relief. I was worried you might be inclined to persuade me to partake in something that was against my personal belief system."

I opened my mouth but all attempts at a witty comeback crash-landed. Who am I kidding? They didn't even take off. Everything in my mind turned to mush. I was so out of my league.

"It smells delicious." He rescued me from having to come up with a clumsy retort.

"Thank you." I stood on his stoop, the hot box pushing the summer's sweltering heat up a few notches.

"I'm honored that you bought me dinner. Do you mind if we eat at the park, though?" He grimaced. "My place is a wreck."

It didn't matter to me where we ate, so long as I got to spend the time with him. If the last few days had taught me anything, it was that I needed to take a step back and not let my obsessive tendencies drive me to the edge. Maybe the one thing I'd been fighting so hard to avoid – a diversion – was what I needed most. "Sure," I shrugged. "I didn't bring any paper plates or napkins though, so I'll have to run back to my place to get some. Is that okay?"

"That'll work," he said, grinning confidently. "Or maybe we should just eat there."

"Sure," I answered.

"Great. I'll grab a couple drinks and meet you there in a few minutes."

I didn't get a chance to peek inside before he pushed the door closed. A rush of adrenaline shot through me. I could only hope that I hadn't crossed the line with my invitation. I had, after all, gone to great lengths to avoid him. It would serve me right if he didn't show up.

I carried the pizza back to my apartment, questioning myself the with every step.

My worries were dispelled before I could even pull plates out of my cupboard.

"Knock, knock." Seth smiled as he pushed the door open.

I was so accustomed to locking things up tight, I jumped at his sudden presence. I fumbled the plates then, in a quick reaction of reflexes, rescued them. "Hey," I said, hoping he hadn't seen my blunder.

"Hey," he smiled back as he set the cold bottles on the counter. "You painted." He nodded at the newly gray wall. "Didn't like the purple, huh?"

"Not really." I shrugged. "Purple's not really my thing." I set the plates on top of the pizza box.

"Oh." He pushed the door closed. "I thought all girls liked purple."

"Well, you thought wrong."

"Noted." He nodded his head.

I added a stack of napkins to the top of the plates. "Do you want to eat on the patio?"

"Perfect." He wrapped his fingers around the neck of both beverages, lifting them with one hand, then picked up the pizza, plates, and napkins from the counter and led me to my patio door.

I pulled the curtain, unlatched the series of locks, and directed him outside.

"You have a nice view," he said as he finished his third piece of pizza.

I assumed he was talking about the sliver of Utah Lake in the near distance and not the parking lot or the stucco walls of the adjacent buildings. I looked over my shoulder to verify. At the beginning of the summer, the lake had been a beautiful blue. Now, in the midst of July, it was a murky green. The locals joked that it was radioactive. I knew nothing of its chemical properties, but as the sun's reflection danced across the water it refracted light into crystalline streaks. There was no denying its beauty.

I turned back to face my dinner companion, wishing I'd blueprinted a list of clever conversation carriers. Instead of talking, I sipped quietly at my drink. With as much plotting as I'd done to start the evening, you'd think I'd have planned something post-pizza-eating. Some date planner I was.

Seth didn't seem to mind the silence. Or the challenge to fill it.

"You missed out on a great run last night," he said.

"Yeah," I swallowed hard. "Sorry about that." He had to have known that I was home when he'd knocked. My car in the parking lot was a dead giveaway.

"I hope everything was okay."

"Yes," I half-lied. "Long day at work. I came home and crashed."

He nodded. "I know how that goes."

I set my drink down and stepped to the patio railing. My patio was shaded by the building as the sun crept westward. His, on the other hand, was full-on drenched in the sun's spotlight.

"I'll bet you can see the sunset from your living room."

"I'm sure I can. I've never really taken the time to notice, though."

He stepped beside me. The closeness of his body sent a quiver rippling through my shoulders and up the base of my neck.

"Did you know that by the time you actually see the sun, it is gone? The same with stars. By time you see some of them, they could already be dead." The comment came out before I had time to process how nerdy I must have sounded. Once they exited my lips, I replayed the words over and over in my mind.

"I didn't know that." He touched my elbow then slid his fingers down my forearm until they intertwined with mine. My body stiffened as he turned me toward him. "Sunsets are pretty spectacular, but the best view I've ever seen is standing right in front of me." His voice, like silk, slid across my entire being. "I want to know everything about you, Ginger."

I gripped the railing with my free hand, wrapping my fingers as if they'd keep me from having a breakdown. His words were meant as a romantic gesture, I know, but frankly, they freaked me out for a minute. Why was he so into me? What if I really was a client?

"Where would you like me to start?" I swallowed hard. My ability to make a sound decision was mired by his hypnotic attention. Hopefully I could spin a lie better than I could keep my growing feelings for him at bay.

"With these eyes." He gently cupped my face. "They're the most exquisite shade of brown. I can't help but wonder where you got them."

The lump in my throat grew to uncomfortable proportions. Could he tell they were contacts?

"Then" – he continued, tracing his thumb over my lips – "I'd like to discuss these lips."

Either I was a sucker or he was good. Real good.

I closed my eyes and let him pull me into him. He brushed his lips across mine, at first with the utmost gentleness and then, as my hesitancy eased, with more fervor.

Never in my wildest dreams had I imagined a kiss could feel so . . . so . . . I was without words. It had been a few years since I'd kissed a guy. Senior year of college, in fact. But Peter Rushton, with his awkward introversion, Einstein-inspired crazy hair, and graphic tees didn't hold a candle to Seth. Really, the only thing about him I'd been attracted to had been his mind. And, if we hadn't been assigned to work together on a Security Foundations project, he'd probably have never looked beyond his dark-rimmed glasses to see that I existed. He was cocky about his computer skills, so much that it became a turn-off. And his kisses . . . well, they definitely never made a surge of elation shoot from my toes to the top of my head. And never had my heart raced and my body quivered in such perfect harmony.

"You know," Seth whispered, "I've liked you from the very first time we met." His hot breath tickled my neck. "And the more I get to know you, the more I realize just how special you are."

Was he for real? "I thought you didn't put much stock in first impressions." My knees and my heart faltered in tandem with each other. The probabilities of us developing into any more than a fling were slim. He didn't really know me.

"You're the exception to almost every rule I have. There's something special about you. You're different than any girl I've met before."

His sturdy arms held me tightly against his strong, chiseled body. If he hadn't held me so tightly, I'm sure I'd have tipped right over. I considered pulling away. Could I really drag him along into my fairytale life? It didn't seem like a fair thing to do.

But then I remembered the pledge I'd made with myself just that morning. I – Ginger – needed to be more spontaneous. I took a deep breath and let go of the rationalizations swirling in my head. I didn't have time to respond before the warmth of his lips pressed against mine again.

I obliged, shedding my inhibitions as I'd never done with any man before. Maybe life as Ginger wasn't so bad. Samantha never felt passion this deeply.

As I melted into him, Seth's phone sounded from his pocket. Without breaking his focus on me, he reached down and silenced it. Immediately, it sounded again.

"Sorry," he whispered to my open lips. The persistent ringing had officially killed the moment. He pulled himself away from me and slipped the phone out of his pocket. "I probably ought to take this." Flashing an apologetic grin, he stepped inside my apartment and slid the patio door shut behind him.

The pattering in my chest slowly fizzled as Seth turned his back to my door and pressed the phone to his ear. I turned my attention to a couple of kids riding their bikes in the parking lot, trying not to eavesdrop on his call. It didn't work. I longed to feel his gentle touch again. What had been so important that he'd felt the need to pull away?

"I think you're making too much of this." His voice permeated through the glass door. "No."

I turned back toward his voice. His body stiffened as his speech became more and more forcible.

"That wasn't a part of the contract." He locked his feet at shoulder distance and squared his free arm behind his back as if striking an at-ease stance.

I refocused my attention on the bicycling kids, wondering why Seth looked so comfortable in a military stance. I was familiar with the pose. It was part of who my dad was. But I couldn't recall Seth mentioning anything about being in the military. He'd told me that he was a business consultant.

A few moments of silence followed then, through the glass, I heard him say, "I'll call you back in five." He stepped back onto the patio. "I'm sorry," he said, wrapping his arms around me from behind. "That was my boss. I'm afraid I've got to go." His lips brushed softly against my cheek then he showed himself to the door.

That night I got two new texts from *The Keeper*. "Keep your head on a swivel," the first text read. They were the exact same words from first time he'd contacted me. Then, "This is no time to break."

I'd anticipated, if nothing else, that Seth would show up at my door at some point the next evening for a run. But, I'd been wrong. Maybe I should've been a little less nerdy with my random science-geek information. Maybe he hadn't felt the same spark I did with our kiss. Or, maybe – probably, actually – the whole thing had simply been too good to be true in the first place.

Trying to blow off the feelings of hurt, I told myself that it was all for the better anyway. I had important work to do. I wondered if that was what *The Keeper* had meant by his warning: *this is not the time break*. Was he – the mysterious voice behind my texts – watching me? And, if so, how much could he see? Could he see me inside my home? Did he know about the night I'd had a breakdown and painted my wall gray? Had he watched me take out my contacts or throw my purple shirt in the trash?

The questions spun through my mind, each seeking an answer. I looked around the room. Other than the picture I'd hung on the wall, there weren't any obvious places to hide even the tiniest of cameras. But that didn't really mean anything. He could still be watching me. Let's face it, he probably was. Or, at least should have been. I wasn't an undercover agent. If the government was invested in keeping me safe, then I could surely hope that they had someone keeping their eye out for me.

But, if he could see inside my apartment, then he clearly knew about my nightly hacking rituals. For months. And hadn't tried to stop me. Or ratted me out.

Or – my mind spun the idea like an old wooden top – had he?

If he'd seen me and ratted me out to Kravitsch, then Kravitsch must not really want me to stop researching. Or he'd seen me and not ratted me out, in which case he – *The Keeper* – thought I should keep working. Or, his reach was limited to things outside my apartment, so he didn't know what I was up to except for what he saw outside the walls of my little home.

Or… the ideas kept spinning. But they all pointed back to one question: what was his basis for thinking I was going to break?

There were so many questions, all of which had answers beyond my reach. There was, however, one thing I could do something about. 43M.

I logged into my servers and dove deep into the dark world of secrets. By midnight I'd filled my notepad with a series of notes, arrows, diagrams, and numbers. To the untrained eye, they'd have looked like nothing more than an incoherent mass of numbers and codes. To me, however, each stroke of the pen and click on my keyboard, represented a step closer to a solution. And, thus, a step closer to getting home.

I knew that the 43M code initiated in Bowling Green, Ohio. I also knew that the attack vector had begun installing on various software channels almost two-months before going live. This was actually a pretty quick implementation. On average, breaches lasted two-hundred days before being found. This wasn't the work of some bored kid. This was someone who had the background and experience to get in and get out quickly and quietly.

I'd found the whats and the hows, but, what I couldn't seem to be able to pin-point the who. Like most hacks, the mastermind had used simple application vulnerabilities to get in, but from Ohio? It didn't make sense. Was the mastermind a domestic terrorist hoping to throw us off his trail by hiding in plain sight? Or was it a foreign entity making his movements – just as I had done – on a secret server thousands of miles away from his keyboard?

I blinked my eyes several times. They were heavy and fatigued from staring at the screen so long. The clock on the bottom of my screen indicated that it was nearly one in the morning. I jotted down a few last notes, so I'd know where to pick up the next day, then logged out.

Stepping to my room, I slid out of my t-shirt and washed my face before realizing that my brain was running too fast for me to simply go to bed. If I had any hope of sleep, I was going to need to silence the chaos.

I put on my running clothes and plugged my favorite classical playlist into my ears then, checking the landing outside my peephole, I stepped into the night.

Dark, heavy shadows hung under the building lights, casting an eerie glow over the grounds of the apartment complex. Even with my music on, the silence outside was almost deafening. Not a single cricket sung or a leaf moved.

I took a deep breath and took inventory of everything in sight. The parking lot was mostly full and only a few apartments weren't dark. I set a comfortable pace down the sidewalk between my building and the neighboring one, taking note of every bush, tree, and shadow along my way.

Deciding to keep my run short, I looped around the deserted pool area and back up between the buildings at the far end of the complex. Just as I approached the common area by Seth's apartment, I heard a sudden bang ricochet off the buildings.

I jumped off the sidewalk and crouched near the bushes, stabilizing myself while I caught my breath. Looking around for the source of the sound, my heartbeat kicked up a notch. A second bang rang out, this time followed by the sound of multiple male voices.

And – I tilted my head to be sure – it sounded like they were laughing.

I held my position in the shadow of the planter as their voices drew nearer. There were two of them, I calculated by the differing pitches of their banter, and they were young. Which meant they were probably fit. My imagination kicked into high gear. What could two, young, fit, gun toting men being doing in the middle of my apartment complex in the middle of the night?

I scooted back between the shrubbery until my back hit the stucco building.

Holding my vigil against the wall, I watched as their silhouettes appeared around the corner of Seth's building. They were tall, definitely young, and . . . and pushing a broken motorcycle.

"Let's try to fire her up again," the boy who was pushing the bike said.

"No way, man," the other guy whispered. "You heard her back-fire back there. The last thing I need is for someone to call the cops."

I released the breath I hadn't realized I'd been holding, and pressed my palm to my forehead. I'd had a freak-out over a back-firing motorcycle.

Holding my position until the boys were out of sight, I made sure no one else was around to witness my stupidity, then slowly climbed out of the bushes. As soon as my feet hit the pavement, I bee-lined it back to my                                    apartment.

# Chapter Eight

The next day, I re-upped my security sweep when I left for work. *Head on a swivel*, I reminded myself with each step I took toward my car. The morning had brought with it a sense of renewal and peace, but I wasn't about to get caught off guard again. Especially with something as stupid as a motorcycle with exhaust problems.

There were six people in the parking lot as I approached my car. Five of them I recognized as neighbors who left about the same time I did each day. The sixth, I'd never seen before. He hovered at the north end of the parking lot, taking long, slow drags off his cigarette as he paced the same three steps over and over again.

I shifted my eyes off of the stranger long enough to notice that Seth's car was gone from its spot. Maybe he'd never even come home for the night. His apartment, after all, had been dark every time I peeked out the curtains. Which was only four times. Okay, five if you count the brief peek from my bedroom window right before falling into bed. Six counting the quick head turn as I'd dashed through the parking lot.

Every time I thought about Seth, an ache formed in my chest. Not only had he not shown up for a run, but there had been no sign of life at his apartment since the night we'd shared a pizza. Was he just giving me a taste of my own medicine? Or had I pulled him into my nightmare? Had I put him at risk?

I wasn't sure whether to be offended or worried.

Clicking the button to unlock my car, I glued my eyes again to the stranger. There was a ruggedness – dirtiness was probably a more appropriate word – about him that didn't fit in with the rest of the clean-cut, semi-rural community. Oily clumps of hair fell across his face then continued down over his shoulders and down to the middle of his back. Deep lines cut out from his eyes and a ratty beard covered his face and down his neck.

The air conditioner blasted as soon as the engine turned over. Twisting the temperature knob down a notch, I fastened my seatbelt and slid the car into gear.

I hesitated for a moment as I shifted the transmission into drive, still taking notes on the out of place man. He wore a long-sleeved flannel shirt – a most interesting choice for a day that was bound to cross the century mark – and knee length cargo shorts. He grinned at me as I drove by, but I didn't return the favor. In my rearview mirror I watched him drop his cigarette butt to the ground, crush it with his toe, then tug his long, dirty blonde hair into a ponytail.

Heat pressed through my windows, though the sun had only crested the mountains an hour before, making the six-minute drive seem like an eternity. The return trip that evening was even worse. I cranked the air conditioner as high as it would go, even though I knew it wouldn't even begin to cool down the passenger compartment of my car before I'd reached my destination. Turning into the parking lot, I noted that the ragged man was no longer lingering, then swept the remaining of the space for anything out of the ordinary.

Tiffanie had just pulled Ian out of his car seat and, settling him on her hip, closed the car door in the spot beside mine. I considered doing a loop around the complex before parking – I'd done a good job keeping my distance from her, or any other neighbors, and I wasn't in the mood to break my streak. But, doing a lap would be an obvious evasion and probably be interpreted as rude. I pulled into my spot and, despite the heat, fidgeted around in the driver's seat until Tiffanie disappeared around the corner and, presumably, into her apartment.

I took another inventory of the complex. No Tiffanie, no smoking stranger… and no Seth. Or at least his car. Though, I'm sure if his car wasn't home, neither was he. It's not like we lived in the middle of a city. Public transportation was virtually non-existent in our little neck of the proverbial woods.

I exited my car and walked the opposite direction of my apartment, noting that all the curtains in Seth's apartment were drawn closed, just as they had been the evening before. I climbed the stairs and, already knowing what the response would be, knocked on his door. Nothing. For good measure, I rang the bell. Twice. Still nothing.

I let out a heavy sigh. Some "friend" he was. He hadn't even said goodbye.

I waited for a short, round man to pass the sidewalk at the base of the stairs before going down them. Sweat pooled under the collar of his cheap business suit as he waddled by. I didn't know his name – had never actually traded any sort of conversation with him – but I knew that he lived around the corner in building G and kept a similar work schedule to mine. We often crossed paths in the parking lot, but he'd barely even noticed me, let alone offered anything more than a curt nod of his head.

The song of a bird sounded from above, drawing my eyes past the security cameras and up a nearby tree. Then back to the security cameras. There were two of them mounted to the top corner of the neighboring building, each pointed a different direction. Looking around the complex, I notice there were several of them.

Rushing to my apartment, I began to form an idea.

If – no, when – I hacked into the apartment's security cameras, I could replay the video feed and see when Seth left. Because knowing this would somehow ease my mind. Not because I was a stalker. I was simply a friend concerned about her friend's safety. Not an obsessed girl. At least not obsessed about him.

My self-justification continued the whole time I tapped into the security feed. Isolating the camera that was aimed at his building was easy. Adjusting its range so that future video would more directly catch his stairs, landing, and door had been even easier.

I rewound the recorded feed, clicking through the twenty-second time lapsed photos at a rapid speed until I found what I'd been looking for. At approximately ten-seventeen the night of our pizza date, Seth had stepped out of his apartment, hopped in his car, and driven away. He hadn't had anything with him to suggest that he would be gone for an extended period of time. Nothing but the clothes on his back and the keys in his hand.

I watched the feed a second time. Then a third. At least he'd left alone, on his own accord, and I could put my worries to rest. The thugs who were after me hadn't gotten to him. But then, where had he disappeared to? And why hadn't he taken anything with him?

I installed a VPN anti-tracker on my phone to block anyone from seeing the app I was about to create and install there. Then I plunked away at my computer until I had created just what I wanted. By the time the sun had disappeared from the sky, my custom app was installed on my phone. As long as the app was turned on, I would receive notification of any movement detected near Seth's front door, courtesy of the apartment manager's security cameras.

I slid my phone into my pocket and dashed over to Seth's stoop to test it out. I knocked on his door, still knowing that there would be no answer, then waited for the ping in my pocket. There was about a forty-five second delay then, just as it was designed to do, the app buzzed through on my phone. I pulled it out and looked at the screen with a grin.

I nearly danced my way down the stairs and back to my apartment, buzzing with the sweet feeling of success. I'd forgotten how good a real hack could feel when it all went as planned. With renewed excitement, I logged into the darknet and resumed my search for 43M answers.

My phone pinged several times over the next twenty-four hours. None of the pictures, however were of Seth. His next-door neighbor came and left seven times – apparently, he kept his schedule busy by juggling three different girls. One of his upstairs neighbors left then returned thirty-minutes later with a small bag of groceries in hand. The other upstairs guy left in the late evening and then returned in the morning. A swing-shifter, I presume.

I was preparing myself for another solo run just after dusk when my phone pinged again. Pulling up the screen, I fully intended to see a snapshot of the little Casanova in F-23, but I was wrong. A man in a dark shirt and plaid shorts stood at Seth's door. His face was hidden under the brim of a baseball hat, but his build was definitely too lanky to be Seth's. Not patient enough to wait twenty-seconds for the next still shot to fill my screen – and knowing that even then it was on a forty-five second delay – I dashed to my patio door and pulled the curtains back just enough to see across the parking lot.

All of Seth's curtains were still closed and the place was completely dark. My phone pinged again, this time showing a snapshot of the man walking through Seth's front door.

I froze. He – whoever he was – was inside Seth's house. Still no lights. I glanced down at the parking lot. Still no car.

My heart pounded and my mind raced to the worst possible place. I backed away from my patio door, letting the curtains fall back into place as I rushed to check my locks. Who was this man? Had he broken in or had he used a key? And where was Seth?

I leaned against my wall and took a deep breath. Then, closing my eyes, took another. Five, I counted to myself. Four. Inhale. Three. Exhale. Two. In. One. Out.

Three minutes later, my phone pinged again. I stared at the screen trying to make out any identifying characteristics about the man as he made his exit. I took a screen shot, saving it on my phone for later reference, then rushed to look out the window again with the hopes of catching him in the parking lot.

There was no sign of movement anywhere in or near the parking lot. Forty-five seconds had apparently been enough lag to help him vanish.

I logged onto my computer and hacked directly into the security cameras again. I rewound the video far enough to watch the man, in twenty-second fragments, approach from between buildings G and H. He kept his hands to his side and skirted along in the shadows before slipping up the stairs in the F building. Even on the video, it was unclear whether he had a key or not. I cursed the cheap apartment management for not having current technology.

The apartment door opened then closed as the man disappeared inside. A few minutes later, it opened again and the man exited in the same, shadow-seeking fashion that he'd arrived in. He kept his hat low and his head turned down. The black and white feed made it hard to identify much of anything other than the guarded way in which he slithered in then out again, as if he were hoping to avoid detection. He slipped back between G and H then disappeared into thin air.

# Chapter Nine

Should I call the police? And tell them what? That I'd tapped into the apartment's security? How about the part where I created an illegal spying app and – potentially – watched someone break into an apartment? I'm sure they'd have been real pleased to find that, even with my spying devices, I didn't actually know whether the man broke in or not. Or perhaps they'd be interested to know that I'm really good friends with the neighbor that lives there but I don't know where he was or even have a phone number so they can give him a call.

I paced back and forth in the kitchen, switching watch between my front door, the live security feed on my laptop, and the dark apartment across the parking lot.

Maybe, I could tell them that some crazy mastermind unit blew up my apartment, sent me into hiding, and now I'm worried that they have my boyfriend/not boyfriend/kissing friend.

Yep. It all sounded pretty legit. They would definitely take me seriously.

Or not.

How would they not think I was crazy? I thought I was crazy.

I kept pacing.

The app on my phone pinged again. F-23's evening entertainment was on her way out. So early? The night had just begun.

I couldn't call the cops, but I needed to bounce my concerns off of somebody. What if Seth had been kidnapped? Or tortured for information? Or...

I started to dial Kravitsch's number then realized he'd have the same qualms that the cops would. I'd hacked into the security system, thus doing the one thing he'd told me would ensure I no longer had a job. And, without a job, I'd likely – I assumed – lose whatever level of protection I was being provided.

"I think I might be broken." I sat on the floor in the corner of my kitchen and sent the words via text to *The Keeper.*

Immediately my phone buzzed back: *Message unable to be delivered. Try again?*

I re-sent it. It didn't go. I re-sent it again. Same return.

I pulled the menu under *The Keeper's* name and selected the call option. I hadn't even put the phone to my ear when the service disconnected. Two words appeared on my screen: *Call Failed.*

I checked the prefix and added a '1' for good measure then tried again.

No ring. Call failed.

I counted again, taking long, deep breaths as I did so. Five. There was no reason to panic. Seth hadn't been in the apartment. Four. His car was gone and I watched him leave on his own, so he hadn't been kidnapped. Three. The intruder went in and out quickly. Whatever he was looking for, he must not have found. Two. He left empty handed. One. He was gone... and I was fine.

I was fine. I rested my head on my knees and repeated the words until my racing heart believed them.

I untied my running shoes and slid them off my feet. After thirty minutes of trying to pound its way out of my chest, a run was probably the last thing my heart needed. I rolled onto my knees then pulled myself up by the kitchen sink. Turning the faucet on, I filled my hands with water and splashed it on my face.

Drawing a few more deep breaths, I deactivated the spying app on my phone then settled in at the kitchen table and opened my laptop back up. I wouldn't be sleeping anyway, I might as well see what dark alley 43M would lead me down.

\*　　　\*　　　\*

When I arrived home from work the next evening, Seth was sitting on the top stair of my landing. He had a DVD in one hand and a bucket of movie theater popcorn on his lap.

"Hi," he said softly.

I stopped at the bottom stair and looked up at him. A buzz shot through me as if I hadn't spent the entirety of the last few days worrying about him. "Hi," I repeated.

He hung his head then locked his eyes on mine somberly. "I owe you an apology."

"For?" I questioned flatly. *For running out on me? Or making me think my 43M thug had gotten you?* My lips remembered the softness of his kiss. *Or kissing me?*

"For the other night. I'm sorry I answered that call, and I'm even sorrier that I let it pull me away."

I processed the apology but didn't answer. If anyone should be apologizing, it probably should have been me. As much as I'd have loved to pursue some kind of forever, it was an impossibility. He was a diversion – nothing more. Stringing him along was unfair to both of us.

"And," he added, "I'm sorry that I've been so busy with work the last couple of days. I've missed running with you." He offered a crooked smile. "Well, actually, I've missed pretty much everything about you."

Smooth. If he was trying to butter me up, he was doing a good job.

It had been ninety-eight hours and fourteen minutes since he'd kissed me. Yes, I'd been counting. I'd missed him, too. But saying the words out loud would imply a level of commitment that I couldn't give. "Where'd you go?" I asked as matter-of-factly as I could, even though I wanted to wrap my hands around his neck and scream the words into his face.

"I got a call from my boss." He shrugged. "Had to catch a last-minute flight." He twisted his mouth halfway into a grin. "When business calls…" He shrugged again. "I'm sorry. I probably should've said goodbye."

"I think I saw someone at your place." I blurted out the words before really thinking about what they might imply.

Not seeming to care that I'd had an eye on his place, he rolled his eyes to the side as if in thought. "Oh, that's right," he answered with a nod. "My friend Jon said he might stop by."

A friend? Since when do friends break in when you're gone? "I think he might have picked your lock and gone inside," I finally say.

"Yep." He shook his head and laughed as if it were nothing. "That'd be Jon."

A friend? I repeated the question to myself. Who snuck in through the shadows, let himself in, then snuck away again? Weird. But, really, not my business. "How did you know that I love movie theater popcorn?" I asked instead of the other questions on my mind.

"Well, who doesn't?" he answered with a wink, all signs of penitence gone. "The real question is, do you like movies?"

I leaned against the handrail, trying to look casual though I'm sure I failed. All I could think about was the fact that he was back—and still interested. "Depends on the movie."

"*Star Wars.*" He lifted the case so I could see the cover. "*Episode IV. The Last Hope.* You know, the original 1977 version. Harrison Ford, Carrie Fisher." He raised a brow.

"It's my favorite," I said genuinely.

"Really?" His eyes lit up.

"Really."

I pulled my key out of my handbag and climbed the stairs. When I passed him, I nudged his shoulder with my hand. "Should we see if my DVD player works?"

"Yes, please." He hopped up from the top stair as I turned my key in the door then followed me inside.

I set my bag on the kitchen table beside my laptop then flipped the notebook over so he couldn't see my notes. Not that he'd understand any of my notations of flow charts, but I was protective of them anyway. Plus, he thought I was a somewhat normal girl. If he knew just how deep of a geek I was, he might change his mind about me.

"There's one more thing." He settled onto the couch as I popped the DVD into the player and pushed play. When I turned around he extended an envelope toward me.

"What's this?" I asked, nodding at his offering.

"Another plea for your forgiveness."

I took the small white envelope and examined it. "You know," I said, sliding my finger under the seal, "you were forgiven as soon as I saw the popcorn."

"Then consider this a deposit for the next time I do something stupid." He smiled and nodded for me to open the gift.

"So, you're saying there's going to be a next time?"

"I'm only human, you know."

I was actually starting to wonder if he was. Heat rushed to my face as I smiled at him.

"Are you going to open it?" He pointed excitedly to the envelope.

Reaching into the open pocket, I grinned down at him then gasped as I pulled out a set of tickets. "Abravanel Hall." My lips trembled as I read the stubs out loud. "For this weekend. Seth, no. This is too much."

His irresistible blue eyes smiled at me as he raised his brows. "I'm assuming that means you like the symphony." The corners of his mouth drew back into a smirk.

"Yes!" I stared at the tickets a few moments longer then threw my arms around his neck. "I love the symphony. How did you know?"

"Lucky guess." He wrapped his arms around me and pulled me onto his lap.

Before Han Solo's Millennium Falcon even got off the ground, my lips were running their own solo mission over Seth's. Suddenly life back in Virginia didn't seem so appealing. I committed to making the most of every short-lived moment I had left with Seth.

\*     \*     \*

Seth was standing on the sidewalk near my parking spot as soon as I pulled in, dressed even more casually than normal in shorts and a t-shirt.

"Hi?" I questioned as I stepped out of my car. The summer sun was a sweltering reminder that, despite the surrounding mountains and nearby lake, we were, indeed, in the desert.

"Hello." He stepped forward and kissed my cheek. "So, I was thinking" – he settled his hands on his hips. "And I don't want you to think that I'm trying to monopolize your time." He shook his head. "Actually," he raised a finger, "that's a lie. I *am* trying to monopolize your time. All of it. I really enjoy being with you."

"Wow." I laughed. "You really know how to lay it on, don't you?" Heat radiated off the asphalt, searing the soles of me feet through my dress shoes.

"Too much?" He raised his brows.

"Nope." I clicked the lock button on my key fob. Neither one of us flinched when the car honked twice. "Feel free to keep it coming."

"I knew you were an attention hog." He stepped back up to the sidewalk.

"Guilty as charged." Dropping my keys into my handbag, I followed him off of the hot blacktop.

"It's always the quiet ones you have to watch out for." He shook his head and smiled playfully. "They're the ones with the most to hide."

He had no idea. I offered a quiet smile.

"So," he pulled his car keys out of his pocket. "Have you been to the aquarium?"

"The aquarium?"

"Yeah. It's just a few miles north of here. They've got all kinds of fishes and stuff."

"Fishes and stuff? Wow, you're quite the salesman."

"I do my best." He pinched the fabric at the base of his neckline and gave it a double tug.

"The aquarium?" I asked again.

"Well, I noticed that picture you hung – the new one of the beach – and figured you must like the beach. And if you like the beach, then you must like the water.

And fishes and stuff live in the water, so you'd probably think it was fun to go look at them."

"Interesting theory."

"Or" – he jingled his keys – "maybe what you're really interested in is just spending time with me. In which case, I will happily accept your companionship in the venue of your choosing."

He could've invited me to the McDonald's Playland and I'd have willingly agreed. "Can I change out of my work clothes before we go see fishes and stuff?"

"That is a valid question." He looked me over. "And, while I think you are smoking hot in that blouse, I know what it's like to be stuck in a collar and slacks all day, so I will oblige you to put on something more comfortable."

"Your thoughtfulness has been noted."

He cupped his hand around the base of my head and leaned down to kiss me. "Go ahead and do what you need to do," he said as our lips parted. "I'll just chill out here until you're ready."

"Okay," I replied as he stepped away to give me room to pass. "I'll be quick."

I nearly raced up the stairs and into my apartment with the intent to change and get back to Seth's presence as soon as possible. I dashed into my room, shedding my blouse in the hallway like a child excited for a special outing, then shimmied out of my dress slacks in a single, fluid motion. I'm sure it was a personal record, if not a world one.

In another feat of wonder, I selected a shirt and a pair of denim shorts out of my closet without so much as a second thought. I practically jumped into the shorts as I slid the shirt over my head then stepped in front of my dresser mirror to make sure everything was in proper place. I tipped my head upside down, ran my fingers through the loose curls, then let my hair fall over my shoulders as I stood back up. A quick shake of my head realigned my part to its proper place. I smeared a fresh coat of lipstick on my lips then, smacking them together loudly, grabbed a pair of comfortable, flat shoes and headed back down my hall.

I almost made it out the door when I noticed the subtle glow seeping out around the edges of my laptop. Curious, I stepped over to my machine and opened it. The monitor was alive and stuck on my password screen.

I typed in my password, still confused as to why the machine hadn't been asleep. Pulling up the settings, I tabbed down to the control center and opened the advanced options screen. As expected, everything was in order. The settings were just as they should've been. Everything was set to power off when the machine's lid was closed.

I mentally ran through other reasons the computer might not have shut down. Had I not closed the lid all the way the last time I'd used it? Unlikely. It's not like it took a lot to swing the lid closed. Maybe it was a hardware failure. Perhaps the graphic card was going out. It was a fairly new machine, but it was a cheap one, so I wouldn't be surprised.

I'd run a more thorough scan when I got back home, but even the worst-case scenario didn't have me overly worried. If someone had tried to hack my machine, they'd have found a clean system. The only chance they'd have of finding anything was if they physically accessed my computer. To do that they'd have had to come in my apartment and tried to log on.

But, that didn't make any sense either. If they'd try to bypass my password, it would've been reset. And it wasn't. I shook off the paranoia. Even if someone had hacked into my laptop, it was simply a dumb keyboard. They wouldn't have found anything. There was nothing on the machine. All my data and search history were on hidden on my secret servers. They were untouchable. I had nothing to worry about.

Exiting out, I closed the lid, waited until I heard the processor shut down.

I double checked the locks on all my windows then looked for signs of forced entry as I walked out my front door. There was nothing out of the ordinary. All was secure.

Determined not to let my imagination get the best of me, I dismissed the computer lights as a fluke and rushed down the stairs to meet up with Seth.

\*        \*        \*

The aquarium was fun, dinner was great, and our six-mile lap around the neighborhood was invigorating. But the best part of the day took place when Seth's lips danced over mine under the glow of my porch light. There was no logic behind it, and I couldn't quantify what was happening to me, but I'd never felt such a draw to anyone before. I longed to be around him with an urgency I didn't fully understand.

"Can I monopolize more of your time tomorrow morning?" I couldn't have looked appealing after a six-mile run, but his eyes danced over mine like he'd found a great treasure.

"Well, I was planning on going dress shopping." I let him pull me close to him, despite the heat radiating from both of our bodies. "Someone got me tickets to the symphony tomorrow night and there's nothing in my closet quite worthy of such an event. But if you'd like to do some shopping…" I smiled up at him.

"Umm, actually…"

I settled my hands on his chest and laughed. "That's what I thought."

He kissed me again. "Concert starts at seven. I'll pick you up just before five."

"Five?" I asked as his lips brushed mine.

"Is that too late?" He pulled away just enough for me to see his grin. "I can do four. Or even three."

"What happened to five?"

He ran his hand up the base of my neck and into my sweaty ponytail. "Two it is."

"Really?"

"On second thought," he traced his finger down my jawline. "Why don't I just go shopping with you?"

I'd always thought I'd be happy in a life of solitude, but now I found myself restructuring that idea. There had to be a paradigm where we could work—Seth and Ginger, Ginger and Seth, Samantha and . . .

Where did Samantha fit into this picture? I wouldn't be Ginger forever. This could be my one shot at true love, and it was based on a lie. Oh, how I hated my life.

# CHAPTER TEN

Second to techno music and *Star Wars* marathons, the symphony was one of my favorite things. Of course, it warranted dropping my Saturday plans with my laptop in favor of an early lunch with Seth and then shopping for a dress worthy of a sophisticated cultural event. It was a sacrifice I was happy to make.

I wasn't much for fashion, but as soon as I saw the black dress in the store window, I was in love. Seth occupied himself in the store while I tried it on. I slid the black fabric over my head then pulled it into position around the curves of my body. It was fancy, but not stuffy. Sexy, yet classy. And definitely not conservative enough for Samantha.

I spun from one side to the other in front of the dressing room mirror, silently thanking Ginger for helping me push out of my comfort zone. I'd come so far from that fumbling, awkward, introvert who'd tossed her frumpy brown cardigan in the trash and hopped on a red-eye just a few months before. And I'd come especially far since bumping into Seth just a few weeks ago. That nervous, paranoid girl in the parking lot was gone – or at least hiding – behind a confident, carefree one.

I spun in front of the mirror again, this time giving credit to Seth for the transformation he'd helped me feel, even if it couldn't necessarily be seen.

The saleslady had helped Seth pick out a coordinating necklace and shoes while I was in the dressing room. They were perfect. I added them to the tab then headed home so I could pull myself together for our first official formal date.

In addition to boosting my self-esteem, my time with Seth had proven to be a nice diversion from my 43M research. I'd needed to step back and take a breather and he'd been a good breather to take. So much so, that I'd almost forgotten that a different part of me existed. My computer had sat, virtually untouched for three days. It was an achievement even I was proud of.

I freshened up my makeup using the same techniques the little ninja lady had shown me, making sure to focus on the very smallest of details. I applied an extra layer of mascara then smacked my bold, red lips together, pleased with my efforts.

Though I was sure I'd pale in comparison to Seth, I wanted to look as good for him as possible. As soon as I saw his face, I knew I'd succeeded.

"Hi." I smiled widely as I opened my front door, feeling confident that my hair and makeup efforts were a good compliment to the black, form-fitting dress. He wore a dark gray suit. It was perfectly tailored to accentuate his strong shoulders and tone torso. A light blue dress shirt with small blue pinstriping peeked out from under the suitcoat, drawing out the blue in his eyes. He'd taken Greek-god-hot to a whole new level.

"Well" – he took my hand and pressed it to his lips – "look at you." I felt his eyes move from the v-cut neckline, over the curves of my torso, then down the sleek lines of the dress. "Stunning."

It was the response I'd hoped for as I'd primped for the latter half of the afternoon, but the compliment still made me blush. I wasn't used to such adulation. But I liked it, so I figured I should cherish it while I had the chance. Sooner or later I'd have to deal with the fact that I wasn't really Ginger, which meant this charade would come to an end. I hoped for a quiet close, but the pang in my heart told me it wouldn't be.

"Are you ready?" He extended his hand in front of him.

"Ready as I'll ever be." I tucked my clutch to my side and settled my hand into his.

In true gentleman fashion Seth wrapped his fingers gently around mine and escorted me to his car. He held the door open and I slid into the front seat, feeling like the princess I hadn't realized I wanted to be. As I watched him walk confidently around the hood, his shoulders square, his chin high, I wondered what the future held for Ginger's identity.

Still assuming 43M was the case that was keeping me at risk, I reconciled the need to connect the missing pieces ASAP. If not for our country's sake, for my own.

Seth's door popped open and he slid inside. He started the car then his hand reached across the console and found mine. I wrapped my fingers around his and, knowing that eventually I'd have to end my charade, held on. After the symphony I would need to reprioritize again, this time putting my research back into urgent status. As much as I'd liked being distracted, my conscience whispered that I was being unfair – unfair to Ginger, unfair to Seth, and completely unfair to Samantha.

If I could find closure with my case before Seth and I got too deep, maybe I'd be okay to walk away. Or—I sighed at the thought—maybe it was already too late. My heart pounded wildly as I watched him out of the corner of my eye. What if he felt the same for me? Would he still want to be with me after I shed the chocolate brown eyes and sassy brunette hair?

I sank deeper into the car's seat, the sad reality flooding over me. What had started as a diversion had turned into something so much more. I had feelings for Seth. Real ones that were growing by the minute. And I wanted them to last beyond tonight, and beyond Ginger. But, was that – the concept of Samantha and Seth – even an option?

I traced my thumb over his. Ginger would likely disappear just as quickly and quietly as she'd appeared. I was certain, however, that my feelings for Seth wouldn't vanish quite so easily. I was also certain that I couldn't keep lying to him. I didn't like lying. Seth deserved more than that.

Seth sung along with almost every song on the radio as we drove over the point of the mountain and continued north into the foothills of Salt Lake City. Bobbing his head, he kept perfect harmony with the beat of the music and smiled at me. He was so many levels of perfect, I couldn't help but smile back. I may have never dared dream about a man like Seth, but as I sat beside him in his car, I knew I had to do whatever I could to hold on to him. If there was any chance of being with him beyond Ginger's run, I had to find it.

I traced my thumb over his again then settled my hand into his open palm. "Thanks, again, for taking me to the symphony," I said.

"It's my pleasure." He wrapped his fingers around mine.

"Actually," I mumbled to myself, "it's mine."

I marveled at the beautiful mountains that towered over the east side of the car, feeling small, yet determined in their shadow. I could do this. There had to be a way. If I could make this – the knee-buckling man, the beautiful mountains, the security, the love – my future, then why had I been so set on running? Had my life back on the east coast been that fantastic?

The answer sat next to me, gently cupping his hand around mine.

The footprint of the entire valley laid out in front of us as Seth pulled into a small, obscure parking lot on the eastern most bench of Salt Lake City. Rolling past a series of small businesses, he stopped the car in front of a rustic Renaissance storefront.

Seth nearly floated around the car, his face covered with a grin, and opened my door. "My lady," he nodded as he offered me his hand.

"Why, thank you, kind sir." I played along.

He pulled me to my feet then, looking over my dress again, said, "Thou dost taketh my breath away."

I tried to muffle my laugh, but it slipped past my lips.

"Am I trying too hard?" He held the restaurant door open for me.

"Maybe just a little." I navigated my black stilettos over the cobblestone path and into the fancy foyer. Heavy cornices and dark, ornately carved crown molding capped the room. A life-sized painting of men in traditional French tights and heavy, fur trimmed coats adorned the wall behind the reservation desk.

The greeter confirmed our reservation then led us through the dimly lit restaurant. An oversized table and two equally oversized chairs waited for us in front of a stained-glass window. Seth wrapped his hands over the sides of the massive chair, his fingers looking small as they held onto the heavy, ornate wood.

"Thank you, kind sir." I settled into the giant chair, feeling tiny in its frame.

"My lady, tis thee I thank." He smirked as he slid into the seat across from me. "But for real," he said, breaking out of his renaissance talk, "isn't this place incredible?"

"Yes." I smiled, counting the line of forks on the table. "Have you been here before?"

"No. The guy I got the symphony tickets from recommended it."

"Well if the food is as good as the atmosphere, I think we're in for a treat."

Five full courses later, I was regretting my decision to wear a figure-fitting dress. Though the portions had been moderately-sized, they'd been plentiful.

Seth pulled my chair out for me then, leading me back to the car, repeated the same phrase he had when we'd arrived. "Thou dost taketh my breath away."

I was starting to think maybe he was as big of a liar as I was. "I believed you the first time you said that, but now I have to wonder if that's just a phrase you practiced."

"Tis not, my lady." He tugged on my hand, spinning me around until I faced him. "I could say it a million times and it'd still be true." He slid his hands around my waist and pulled me in until our bodies touched. "You are so beautiful." There was a tenderness in his tone that made me believe him. "And I'm so glad that chance brought our paths together."

I absorbed his kiss. Too bad that same chance that brought me to Utah was eventually going to push me back to the other side of the country. Unless... I allowed myself to get swept away by the tenderness of his lips. Unless I came up with a plan B.

\*     \*     \*

"Can you take our picture?" a young girl asked as we entered the balcony at Abravanel Hall. She couldn't have been a day older than seventeen. Even so, her dress hugged the curves of her torso then elegantly ruffled down her legs and onto the wood floor. I longed for just a fraction of her confidence.

"Sure." I smiled at the way she seemed lost in her date and wondered if that's what people saw when I looked at Seth. I'd never understood the whole hopeless romantic thing, but I was beginning to.

"Thanks," she said after I snapped the photo of her and her tuxedoed date. "Do you want me to take your picture?"

I looked at Seth for his approval – secretly hoping he'd have an excuse not to. I'd actively avoided pictures for most of my life, but especially for the last several months, but something inside me really wanted one today. I juggled my feelings. I wanted to document our night out, but at the same time, I wondered if it was a wise thing to do. What if he posted it on one of his social media sites? There were plenty of ways to reverse search an image.

"Sure," he shrugged. "Why not?"

"Great," the bubbly girl chirped. "Do you have your phone?"

Seth nudged me gently. "My phone's mostly for work stuff. Why don't we use yours, Ginger?"

Mine was strictly for work stuff. I hadn't even shared my number with Seth. I didn't argue, though. If it was reverse imaging I was worried about, then my phone was the safest place to keep it. I may have removed the spy app but I still had the VPN anti-tracker installed. And I most definitely wasn't going to share it anywhere. Ginger didn't even have a social media account.

Pulling my phone out of my small, silver clutch, I opened the camera app, and handed it over to the chipper young lady then stepped beside Seth. He settled his arm over my shoulder and offered his most mesmerizing smile.

"Smile," the girl exclaimed as she positioned my phone's camera on us. Seth leaned in and kissed my cheek just as the flash erupted. "Perfect," she squealed.

"Thanks." I smiled as I took my phone back from her. Seth looked over my shoulder and we both reviewed the snapshot. I did a doubletake at the shot. I barely recognized myself. I looked surprisingly confident and sexy.

Satisfied, I dropped my phone back into my clutch and took my seat. If nothing else, at least I had proof that this night had been more than just a dream.

By the end of the symphony's third movement, I'd decided it was time to stop secretly driving the 43M research forward. It was eventually going to work out without my help, but as much as I'd wanted to be free of Ginger, I didn't want to be free of Seth. But then what? If I disconnected my servers and tucked my black hatting away, what would happen when the case was solved? Would the government automatically send me home or would I be allowed to stay?

I needed to contact Kravitsch. If I had any hope of picking my own path and embracing the possibility of a *real* relationship with Seth, we had to have a plan in place. I rehearsed the conversation over and over in my head.

"Are you okay?" Seth turned the volume down on the radio and pulled me from my thoughts. For the better part of our drive from Salt Lake back to Saratoga Springs, I'd been silently working out the prospect of assuming my real identity and then staying in Utah. What might that mean for Seth and me? Could we really have a future? Especially when he found out that I wasn't who I claimed to be?

"Just thinking." I smiled. Happy, glorious, rose-colored thoughts.

Reaching across the console, he rested his hand on top of my knee. "Something serious?" he asked.

"I hope so." Oh, yes, I hoped so.

He reached for my hand then pulled it to his lips and kissed it tenderly. "Well, then I hope so, too."

He notched the volume of the radio back up and resumed singing to each song that came on. I was grateful for his love of the lyrics, as it allowed me to easily slide back into my thoughts.

Seth pulled the car into his assigned parking spot then turned off the engine and made his way around to the passenger side door. Taking my hand into his, he helped me out of the car, and we began to make our way toward my apartment.

"Did you leave a light on when we left?" His voice tensed.

It didn't seem plausible. The sun had been high in the sky when we'd left, but as I looked up at the kitchen window, light radiated from behind the drawn blinds.

"I must have," I answered as thoughts of my previous apartment played through my mind. And then I remember his so-called friend, Jon.

Cautiously, we ascended the stairs. I thought of Jon. And 43M. And my old apartment. My heart pounded against my chest, gaining urgency with each step that we took. Each stair that we ascended edged us closer and closer to what I knew could be a potential disaster. Memories of my old apartment's fiery demise halted me at the door. The porch light cast its amber hue over us, hopefully hiding the color that I'm sure had drained from my face.

"Let me go in first." Seth squeezed my hand a single time.

I feigned a grin. "You don't need to do that. I'm sure it's fine." I didn't want him to walk into trouble. My trouble.

Trying to mask my nerves, I fished my key out of my clutch. Before I could stop him, Seth swiped it from my hand. He slid it into the lock then cautiously stepped inside. I followed closely behind, wondering if this might be a good time to fill him in on my history.

"Stay right here," he quietly instructed as his eyes scanned the tiny kitchen and living area. "I'm going to go check the bedroom."

The palpitations in my chest became almost audible as I watched Seth move down the short hall. Drawing in a deep breath, I took comfort that there was no smell of gas in the air, then inventoried the living area. Everything seemed to be in order. My TV remote sat squarely on the coffee table, my breakfast dishes still by its side. My laptop, too, sat in its rightful place on the end of the dining table. If someone—whether it be a petty thief or a 43M thug—had been in my apartment, surely that would be the one thing they'd have taken.

I stepped up to the table and touched the laptop's lid, still confused by the light over the sink. Maybe I'd left it on the night before. I began to chronologically classify my movements from the previous evening just as Seth's strong arms wrapped around me from behind.

"All clear." He breathed the words warmly on my neck as his hands settled on my hips.

My panicked nerves settled with each tender kiss on my ear lobe. He cupped my hands in his then traced his lips along the curve of my jaw and onto my neck. A pulse of energy ran through me as I melted into him.

I would definitely be calling Kravitsch first thing in the morning.

# Chapter Eleven

I startled awake at the sense that I wasn't alone. It had been hours since I bid Seth a passionate goodbye and locked the door behind him, and yet, in the silence of my bedroom, an uninvited presence lingered. A chill coursed up my toes then settled on my shoulders. Pulling my blankets up, I knotted them at the base of my neck and rolled over in the darkness.

"What in the . . ." I recoiled my body into a protective ball and gasped at the shadow beside my bed.

A suffocating hand fell over my mouth. It was heavy. Strong. "Shh," came a deep whisper as my eyes began to focus in the darkness.

I recognized the voice. "Seth?" I mumbled through his flesh.

He kept one hand firmly over my mouth as he drew the other up. Raising a finger to his lips, he whispered softly, "Don't talk. Don't question. Just get up as silently as you can and follow me."

I squeezed my eyes closed then opened them again. The lustful dream he'd pulled me from had me hoping that his intentions were passion driven, but the aggression in his tone suggested otherwise. "But . . . what . . ." The incomprehensible words muffled into his hand.

"No questions." He leaned in and breathed the words into my ear. The heat from his breath settled heavily over my skin. "Please, just do what I say."

I swallowed hard, wondering how I'd so grossly misread the situation. Hadn't I, just hours before, been basking in his passionate kisses?

I didn't budge.

"Listen, *Samantha*" – he moved his hand off my mouth and grabbed my shoulders – "I'm not playing games here." His eyes locked mine with a seriousness I didn't dare refute.

I don't know if it was fear that he knew my real name or the sudden feeling that he'd been playing me all along, but I felt moisture form in my eyes. This was no time for tears.

My jaw tightened and my hands began to shake. Sucking in a deep breath, I let it out again then swallowed the lump that had formed in my throat. I was confused and scared at the same time. *What was going on?*

I had no idea but, clearly, I needed a plan.

Seth pushed a t-shirt and a pair of jeans at me with a nod. Figuring being dressed was a good first step to any plan, I scooted to the edge of the bed and, feeling strangely disoriented, held my blankets tightly up to my chin.

He held vigil beside me, waiting for me to slide into the clothes.

"Listen." He leaned over and pressed his face close to mine after several moments. "If you don't want to get dressed," he breathed the words quietly, "that's fine with me. If you want to come in this" – he traced his fingers softly over the thin strap of my camisole – "I'm not going to argue. But whatever you're going to do" – he was so close to my face I could feel him breathing – "you've got about five seconds to do it." His eyes locked with mine for an intense moment then he stood back up and, jostling his attention between me and the bedroom door, took a step back.

Five seconds. What could I do with five seconds? I could roll to the other side of the bed, dash to the window, and jump out. Or I could test out my self-defense training. Maybe I could kick him in his jaw hard enough to buy me enough time to escape out the front door. Or, perhaps, I could sit frozen on the edge of the bed.

"Three seconds." Seth reached behind his back and slid his hand beneath the bottom hem of his shirt.

In a somewhat half-glazed, not-quite-awake mode, I kept my eyes on him and continued to contemplate my options. Could I dash under his arms and quickly run past him?

He stood erect and alert as his eyes shifted around the room. He looked from the door to the window, back at me, then to the door again.

He stared out my door and into the darkness. "Time's up," he said as he drew a gun from the back of his pants, grabbed my arm, and pulled me to my feet. "Let's go," he demanded, sinking his fingers into my bicep.

My mind couldn't process everything quickly enough. Seth. In my room. With a gun.

I grabbed the jeans as he dragged me toward the bedroom door. "Please?" I lifted the pants in front of me. My hands were shaking. He paused in the doorway and, focusing his attention on the hallway, allowed me to quickly wiggle my way into the stiff cotton. Still trying to compute what was going on, I grabbed my cell phone off the corner of the nearby dresser and slyly tucked it into my back pocket before he pulled me down the hall.

When we reached the kitchen, Seth paused for a moment in the darkness, readjusted his grip on my arm, then slowly moved us to the door and peered out the peephole. Smoothly, he pulled the front door open just enough for us to slip through it then closed it quietly behind us.

"Seth?" I demanded information. "What's going on?" My lips tremored.

He raised the gun and touched the barrel to his lips as a reminder that he wanted me to remain silent. I respected his plea on the pure qualification that he held a firearm, though my stomach became more and more unsettled by the second.

Moving swiftly down the stairs, we quietly skirted around the back side of my building, and away from the parking lot. An owl hooted in the distance. I clenched my teeth and held my breath. Then there was a pop. And a hiss. Then the choking of smell of irrigation water as the sprinklers spat to life. Seth moved us around them and, hugging the shadows between building C and B, maneuvered us into the guest parking lot.

"Get in," he ordered as he pulled the door to an old Chevy Camaro open and nudged me toward it.

My bare feet scraped against the asphalt as I sized up the car. It was an eighties model Z28 with a scoop on the hood and a spoiler on the rear. Jet black and polished to the hilt. Just the kind of car my dad would've gone nuts over. And the kind people don't just lend out to each other. "Whose car is this?"

"Just get in," he ordered again, this time with more force.

"No." Small rocks stabbed at my soles as I anchored my feet to the pavement. "Not until you tell me what's going on."

"Now is not the time to doubt me." The words came out with a sense of urgency as his eyes darted around the dark parking lot.

My throat grew increasingly tight but I still didn't move.

"NOW, Samantha." The command rumbled through his throat, dry and rude. He thrust the gun in my ribs. "Get in the car, NOW!"

My eyes glazed over as he used my real name for a second time. There was only one way he'd know it. The pressure of the steel barrel and the rush of his commands motivated me to slide into the passenger seat.

"Don't even think about trying to run," he warned.

Tears rolled down my cheeks as he slammed the door. I reached for my phone hoping to dial 911 before Seth made it to the driver's seat. He moved too quickly though. I shoved the phone down my cleavage as his door swung open.

Seth slid into the driver's seat, transferred the gun to his left hand, and reached for my chest. Four hours before I might have welcomed the movement, but as I sat in the dark parking lot, feeling violated, angry, and scared, I slapped at his hands. Undeterred by my protests, he fished down my shirt. I clawed at his arms as he pulled out my phone.

"What are you doing?" I punched him several times in the arm. He didn't flinch. I wondered if I could move fast enough to get the gun from him. But then what? Could I use it before he was able to muscle it back away from me?

He backed the sports car out of the parking lot then, taking advantage of its board-out engine, sped toward the highway. While he drove, he slid the back off my phone, yanked at something inside, and tossed all the pieces out the window.

"Thanks!" I yelled. "That was a new phone," I snarled.

"Not new enough."

I studied the gun again, weighing my options and considering ways to get it. "Where are you taking me?" I demanded. Of all the questions swimming through my mind, why had I chosen that one? Apparently, Seth wondered the same thing.

"I call you by your real name and pull a gun on you, and *that's* what you're worried about?"

"Fine," I scoffed, hating him more and more by the minute. "How do you know my name?" I crossed my arms over my chest and pressed my back into the aged leather seat.

"Does the name Rushton mean anything to you?"

Peter Rushton? My college boyfriend? "Not really," I lied. A small, hard rock formed in my throat.

"I think it does." He glared at me. "Senior year at MIT? Ring any bells?"

I shook my head.

"Perhaps it'll come back to you." Raising a disbelieving brow, Seth rushed on, "Just over a year ago Rushton launched a computer security firm in Indiana. Just a small shop with a few employees. They were in the process of developing some patch management software. Anti-hacking type of stuff. You'd know more about that than I do. I don't really talk geek."

"And?" I didn't see how this applied to me.

"He recently hired me to find you. Why do you suppose he did that?"

Rushton had always been an odd guy—introverted and socially awkward. Not that those two qualifications were out of the ordinary for a computer geek. And he was from Fort Wayne, Indiana, so it made sense that he'd open a shop there. Hardly newsworthy. I had no idea what he wanted with me. Unless . . .

My 43M research nudged my conscience. There had been something familiar about the coding. Something I hadn't been able to put my finger on. Could it be Rushton? My shoulders stiffened and the air got thick.

I looked around, reevaluating my exit options. I couldn't help but look at Seth. Now I understood why he'd been too good to be true. "You're a hit man? And I'm a job?" The realization made me sick. "You" – I breathed deep, trying to calm my nerves. Five. In. Four. Out. Three . . .

"Rushton realized someone" – he raised a brow and tipped his head toward me – "was getting close to hacking into his business. He didn't like it. He thought you might be a threat, so…" Seth's knuckles whitened around the steering wheel. It was the only sign he'd shown of any stress. "So," he took a deep breath, "he had me bug your phone and computer. But most of all, he wanted me to get inside your head. Find out how much you knew."

"Well isn't that fantastic!" I yelled. I was angry. Angry at Seth. Angry at myself. How had I missed the details about Peter? And, how had I allowed myself to drop my guard for a guy like Seth? "Why didn't you just shoot me that first day in the parking lot and be done with it?"

"That was never part of the job." He didn't break his focus from the road.

"And making me fall for you was?"

Silence.

I analyzed the shoulder of the road, wondering if I could jump far enough to miss the asphalt and land in the weeds. Even if I missed, I decided, it would be better than staying another minute in a car with a dangerous, cocky, self-righteous jerk like Seth. I unbuckled my seatbelt and reached for the door handle.

"Sam." He grabbed my arm.

"Don't touch me." I jerked away and pulled the handle. The heavy metal door sprang open, barely missing the ground. Heat radiated up from the asphalt. Just beyond the white line, tall strands of dry grass blurred by.

I twisted my torso and prepared to jump.

Seth hit the brakes. Hard. Then swerved the car to the side of the road. The momentum threw me forward. My head smacked the dash. Pain rushed through my head and my vision went blurry.

"I'm sorry," Seth said, pulling me back until my head settled in the headrest. He pushed my hair off my forehead and traced his hand over my cheek. "I don't want to hurt you."

He pulled something from his pocket and took hold of my arm. The last thing I remember was the poke of a needle.

# CHAPTER TWELVE

I lifted my hand to shade my eyes from the bright light in the room. The smell of stagnant sheets and mildewed carport assaulted my senses, though the divot that my body had created in the mattress suggested that I'd been in the room for a long time. Dull pain stabbed the left side of my head, making me want to close my eyes again. My neck was tight and my whole body was stiff and achy like I'd been hit by a bus.

"Are you hungry?" Seth's voice cut through the buzzing inside my head.

"What do you care?" Rolling my neck from side to side, I tried to abate the grogginess, then pressed my hand to my forehead. Suddenly reminded of the tender spot, I traced my fingers over the fresh scab. The dashboard had left a pretty decent gash just above my left eye.

"I know you don't want to believe me, but I'm really not the bad guy here."

I ran my hand over the injection site at the top of my arm. A small, red dot marked the point of entry, but at least it didn't hurt. Clasping my hand over it, I mimicked the movement with my other hand, crossing my arms over my chest and hugging my bare shoulders.

"You're a hired gun." My fury was intensified as I noted his position by the hotel room door. He sat arrogantly in a ragged old chair, gun positioned between his thigh and his right hand. "Please help me understand how that qualifies as anything but bad."

"I'll admit I've had some shady dealings in the past." He sat up taller, with an air of confidence, but didn't move his hand from the pistol. "But this is different. You are different."

"So I've been told." I managed to sit up and scoot to the edge of the bed. The curtains were drawn closed, but through a small sliver in them, I caught the crimsons and golds of the setting sun. Whatever he'd shot into my arm had knocked me out for the better part of the day.

"It's the truth."

"The car?" I bobbed my head toward the window. I could see just enough of the front fender to know that the classic Z28 sat just beyond the hotel room door. "Whose is it?"

"Don't know." He shrugged. "Borrowed it from a dealer's lot in Lehi. It'll be back before they even realize it's gone."

"You stole it. That's classy." I shook my head in disgust. I really knew how to pick them. First Peter Rushton now Seth.

"Samantha, I'd like a chance to explain."

"And I'd like for you to leave me alone." I ran my hands over my eyes and, avoiding the new wound on my forehead, pushed my fingers back through my hair.

"Will you at least hear me out?"

I anchored my feet on the dingy carpet and leaned on the edge of the bed as my legs stabilized. "The last thing I want to do is listen to another lie from your mouth. If you're not a bad guy, then let me go." I started towards the door.

"I can't do that." He took hold of the gun as he stood then raised his hands as if in surrender. "Please." He lowered his arms and tucked the pistol into the back of his pants. "Just trust me."

"Not in this lifetime," I asserted, trying to push him out of my way.

"You don't understand." He wrapped his arms around me and pressed my arms to my torso so I couldn't move them. "I'm not the only operative Rushton hired."

"*Jon*, I presume?" I never believed his cockamamy story about them being friends. Clearly, I'd been wrong.

"That's not really his name, but yes."

"Great!" I wiggled with all the strength I had. "When should I expect not-Jon to arrive?"

"Samantha." He traced his hands up my arms and settled them on my shoulders. "Look at me, please."

I tried to avoid his gaze. I wanted nothing to do with the eyes of a liar. He touched my chin and gently nudged it upwards until my eyes met his.

"Yes, I was hired by Rushton. And yes, I started out thinking this was just another job. But then . . ." His face softened. "Then I started to fall in love with you."

"Shut up!" I thumped my fists on his chest and backed away. He'd roped me in with his charm once. It wouldn't happen again. "Your lies and flattery aren't going to work on me. Whatever information Rushton thinks I have, he's wrong." My jaw tightened with each heated word.

"But he's not. We've been watching you for weeks, listening to your phone conversations, tracking your movements." He paused then added. "Rushton intercepted your emails to David Carey."

I stumbled backwards at the claim. "Impossible," I fumed. "I always use a secure server." I shook my head. "No. There's no way. It's impossible."

"You remember that he's a security genius, right? A hacker, just like you? He knows you – probably intimately" – he flinched at the statement. "Not that

that… Never mind. My point is, he's seen your work. He knows your MO. If anyone can get past your security, it's him."

I considered his words, wanting to refute that who I had, or hadn't, been intimate with was none of his business, but got stuck thinking about the information I'd sent to David instead. None of it was incriminating or detailed, but if Peter had seen it, then he'd have reason to believe I was on my way to piecing everything together. I didn't know how close I'd gotten, but clearly close enough to make him feel threatened.

"What does he want from me?" I crossed my arms tightly across my chest, reminding me that all I had on was a thin, spaghetti strapped, camisole. Wishing I'd grabbed the t-shirt he'd thrown at me – or at least a bra – I turned back toward the bed.

Seth settled his hand on my shoulder. If it'd been any other day, any other situation, I'd have buckled under his touch. "Initially," he started evenly, "all he wanted to do was make sure you weren't digging up stuff he didn't want you to find. The last thing he wanted was for you to stick your nose into his business and shut him down."

"I've got nothing." I pushed his hand away.

"But you do. You've been one step away from putting it all together since I arrived and that's . . ." His tone softened. "That's why he sent me. And when you kept digging and getting closer and closer to him . . ." He moved alongside me and sat on the edge of the heavy dresser then, rubbing his hands up and down his thighs, he added, "When it became apparent that you were a true threat, he ordered me to take you out." He shifted his eyes down at the floor. "Rushton issued the kill order last week." He swallowed hard then added, "When we were eating pizza. On your patio."

"Great!" I turned toward him and threw my arms up in the air. He'd already shattered my heart and destroyed my ability to trust, I might as well let him finish the job. "Then do it already. Put me out of my misery!"

"I don't want to kill you." His hand followed my stare to the gun tucked behind his back. He ran his fingers over the handle of the pistol. "This isn't what it looks like."

I shook my head and moved back toward the bed. "It never is." The sarcastic quip slid easily past my lips as I sat down.

"I love you."

"Clearly," I guffawed, growing more and more irritated every time he said it.

"Will you please let me explain?"

"No," I answered curtly. "I don't think I can handle another lie today." I laid down, rolled over to face the back wall, and curled into a ball. Even the yellowed stripes of peeling wallpaper were better than looking at *him*.

"Not today or ever, for that matter," I added before letting the tears silently spill over my cheeks.

"Please, Sam?" he tried to start explaining again. I pulled a pillow over my head and shut him out. I didn't want to hear another word from him. Ever.

*        *        *

I don't know how long we sat there in silence, but it was fully dark outside by the time Seth spoke again. "Looks like your ride is here." He sat on the edge of the bed and, touching my cheek softly, stirred me awake.

I let the warmth of his fingers settle through me before I snapped back to reality. "My ride?" I asked as I flinched away from his touch. "Where am I going?"

He slowly retreated. "I don't know."

Checking his gun at the small of his back, he made his way to the door. He undid the series of locks that separated the two of us from the outside world then pulled the door open and slid out. He left the door open a crack and I could hear mumbled talking just beyond it.

Seth pushed the door back open and stepped inside. The silhouette of a large, muscular man filled the doorway behind him. It wasn't until the light hit the man's face that I recognized him. Andre. The security agent who'd escorted me out of Kravitsch's office and into my new identity.

I bit down on my lip as Andre walked farther into the room. Suddenly, I regretted not having given Seth the chance to explain. Either Andre had gone rogue, or . . .

"Here," Seth said as he shrugged out of his t-shirt and handed it to me. "You might be a little more comfortable in this." His fingertips lightly brushed over the camisole strap that lay across my shoulder.

The scent of his cologne filled my nose as I pulled the shirt over my head. "Thanks," I murmured.

"I meant what I said," Seth offered as I brushed by him in the open doorway. He reached out and gently touched his hand to mine.

I made the mistake of looking back at him as I walked away. I didn't realize a heart could be twisted and broken so many times in the course of a single day, but as Andre closed the car door and Seth became a shadow in the rearview mirror, I felt what was left of mine disintegrate.

# Chapter Thirteen

Andre purchased me a bagel from the concession stand at the airport before we boarded a red-eye back to Maryland. It did little to soothe the pang in my gut. Likewise, the realization that Seth had driven me from Utah to Nebraska before stopping at that grimy hotel did little to help put things in perspective.

Was he a good guy or a bad one? Had he kidnapped me or saved me?

And had he really meant those three little words?

It took the better part of the day for Kravitsch to debrief me once we arrived back at NSA Headquarters. His explanation of events lined up perfectly with the information Seth had given me. Honestly, I'm not sure why he or the other two guys in black suits felt the need to run through such a thorough—and repetitive—series of questions. It was apparent that they'd already received the bulk of the information they needed to shut Rushton down. What wasn't apparent, however, was who had provided it to them.

"Take the next few weeks off," Kravitsch said as he pulled a set of keys out of his desk drawer. I immediately recognized the gray and red lettering of my MIT keychain.

"And where am I supposed to go?" I asked, taking the nearly forgotten keys from his hand. Had they really held on to my Mini Cooper all this time?

"I don't know," he shrugged. "Wherever you want, I suppose. You've done more than your fair share of overtime these last few months. Take a breather. Decompress."

"But," I started to protest. The last thing I wanted was time to dwell on Seth. I didn't need to relax or think. I needed to keep busy.

Kravitsch raised a definitive finger to block my refute. "We've issued a warrant for Rushton's arrest and expect to have him in custody in the next couple of days. In the meantime, we've got field agents all over him. We can put a security detail on you, too, if you'd like, but I don't think you'll need one."

"I'll be fine," I murmured, though the words were empty.

"Good. Call me if you change your mind."

I nodded.

"You've got three weeks, Perry. Try to enjoy it. And when you're done, you can resume your employment at the Maryland office." He pulled the remainder of my personal belongings out of his desk and handed them to me.

My thumb trembled with relief as I ran it across my employment badge. Things hadn't come to fruition quite like I'd expected them to, but the end result had been the same. Anxious to put Ginger behind me, I followed Andre's lead to the parking garage to retrieve my car. He waited for me to start it up then gave me a curt nod and walked away.

Settling my hands on the leather steering wheel, I sucked in a big breath of the humid air, then collapsed into sobs. After keeping my emotions at bay all day, they flowed out with a vengeance. I'd gotten what I'd been working so dedicatedly towards for nearly five months, I should have been jumping for joy. But, as the tears rolled over my cheeks and off my chin, I succumbed to the feelings of loss that can only come after having experienced love. I felt angry and hurt and . . . and betrayed.

A loud sob pressed up my chest and out my throat. I'd been so careful with my heart and yet . . . the only two men I'd ever given it to betrayed me.

Mopping the tears off the base of my chin with my forearm, I rolled the convertible top down, pulled the brown contacts out of my eyes then, tossing them out the window, put the transmission in drive.

Two hundred miles and just over three hours later, I pulled into the driveway of the only place I wanted to be. I put the car in park then glanced at my reflection in the rearview mirror. I'd allowed my brown hair to blow freely for the entirety of the trip. It was twisted mess of crazy knots. But I didn't care. And neither would anyone else. Shutting off the engine, I slid out of the seat and headed up the walk to the porch.

My first knock yielded no movement from inside the modest bungalow. After knocking a second time, however, a shadow moved through the house. The living room blinds parted, revealing the tips of grease stained fingers. Seconds later, I heard the snap of the deadbolt unlatching.

The door swung wide open. "Samantha?" A set of broad shoulders and a soft belly filled out a set of greasy overalls. He pushed his ball cap off his forehead then, looking me up and down, cracked a smile.

"Hi, Daddy," I sighed as tears began to warm my eyes again. He settled his hand on my shoulder and pulled me into him. I buried my face in his chest and let my tears soak the shirt of the only man I knew would never hurt me.

# CHAPTER FOURTEEN

Over the next week I watched from my parents' couch as the media grabbed hold of PumpPurge and turned it on its head. A live newscast streamed from the TV as federal prosecutors slapped cuffs on Peter Rushton, seized his computer equipment, and slid him into the back of an unmarked FBI car. He didn't look well. His hair, though it'd always been a mess, was longer and scragglier then I'd ever seen it. A graphic tee – so dirty it looked like he'd worn it for several days – hung raggedly over his slim shoulders. His innocent, child-like face was buried behind a knotted beard and his scrawny legs looked like they could barely support the bulge that had formed around his belly.

Peter shielded his face as the news cameras pressed to invade his personal space and for a minute my heart ached with a pity I didn't know I held for him. What I really should have felt was the satisfaction of resolution. I should've been relieved that 43M was finally going to be behind me, but as one day after another slipped by, I couldn't kick the emptiness in my chest.

Somehow, I'd thought getting rid of the brown hair would magically throw me back into my old routine. But it hadn't. Trading the brunette for my natural ginger had done nothing to soften the blow of the Ginger I'd left behind. Whoever invented sabbaticals should have been shot.

Eleven long, torturously boring days after resuming life as Samantha, I thrilled to see Kravitsch's number on the caller ID of my parents' land line.

"Perry." He wasted no time getting to the point. "I just wanted to verify that this was the best number to get ahold of you."

"Yes," I said, disappointed that he wasn't calling to tell me I could come back to work early. I needed motivation. A purpose to get dressed in the morning. A reason to quit feeling sorry for myself.

"Good. Things are wrapping up quickly. An attorney with the USDOJ will be calling you shortly." He hung up without so much as a goodbye.

Minutes later the phone rang again.

"Miss Perry," a strong, deep voice buzzed through the line. "I'm Mr. Jasper Banks, the federal attorney assigned to the PumpPurge case."

"Great." The word slid past my lips without even a hint of excitement.

"I have a lot of information to go over with you about the case." He paused for a moment then added, "And Peter Rushton. I've set aside a few hours to meet with you on Thursday. Ten-thirty in my offices."

He didn't bother to ask if that time worked for me before reciting the address and brief directions to his office.

"What if I had plans?" I grumbled to the kitchen walls as I hung up the call from Mr. Banks. Plans, for instance, like wasting another day on my parents' couch, eating ridiculous amounts of pistachios, watching mindless TV, and redissecting everything with Seth. Plans to reevaluate—for the umpteenth time—my anger, frustration, confusion, and ultimately longing for a man who'd hunted me down and used me.

"Who was on the phone, dear?" Mom pulled the garden gloves off of her hands and tucked them into her pocket as she walked in to the kitchen. Her hair was pulled into a messy bun at the back of her head. A baseball hat, complete with a giant red B above the rim, capped off her gardening ensemble. It was the only connection she still held to her childhood in Boston.

"The federal prosecutor," I shrugged. "He wants to meet with me on Thursday."

Mom settled her hand on my shoulder. "That's great sweetheart. I'll bet it will be nice to get this all behind you."

What she really meant was that she was glad I'd have a reason to take a shower and get out of my pajamas.

"Yeah, it is." I opened the fridge and stared inside as if it had the answers to putting my heart back together.

\*     \*     \*

Two days later, obediently following Mr. Banks' instructions, I made the drive back to Maryland to officially log my affidavit with the court. I parked my car in a nearby public lot and took the time to drink in the Maryland landscape as I walked to the courthouse. Maybe it was the sweet smell of home, or perhaps it was the promise of getting my life back, but with each step my heart soared.

And then it stopped.

The breadth of his shoulders in a suit coat was hard to ignore as he exited the building and confidently made his way across the courtyard. There was no breeze but that didn't stop me from imagining his blond hair dancing the same way I knew his eyes did.

"Seth?" His name tickled its way across my lips as barely more than a sigh.

"Seth?" I questioned again, this time it was actually audible. I rushed toward the curb where a taxi was rolling to a stop in front of the man. Maybe I'd confused his identity with someone else.

My breath stalled as he squared his shoulders and crossed his arms behind his back. If it wasn't him, the resemblance was uncanny. He bent down and addressed the cabby through the passenger window then moved toward the back door.

"Seth?" This time I nearly yelled it.

His hand froze on the cab's door handle.

"Seth?" I called again, this time with a tremble in my voice.

He pulled the car door open then paused again. A smile painted its way across his face as he turned to face me. "Samantha."

"I . . ." What do you say to a man who was supposed to have killed you but instead professed his love?

"You're absolutely stunning as a ginger." Filling the conversational void, he stepped toward me and fingered my red curls.

"Thanks," I said, glad to be back to my natural color. Swallowing the resurfacing fear that he'd never really felt for me what I had for him, I looked up into his eyes. "I'm sorry I didn't give you a chance to explain."

"No apology needed. You had no reason to."

"I'd like to hear it now." The words flew boldly past my lips. I wanted to believe that behind those eyes was something more than a man who'd played me.

"I'm guessing now isn't really a good time for you." He eyed the courthouse.

I didn't care if I sounded desperate. I wanted resolution. Needed it. "How about after my meeting? Maybe we could grab some lunch."

"I don't think that's a good idea."

"Why?" I asked though I felt he'd already confirmed my suspicions. I answered for him. "Because it really was a lie, wasn't it?" My heart sunk. I turned to walk away.

"No." He gently grabbed my arm and turned me back around. "It's . . ." He sighed and looked over his shoulder at the waiting taxi. "I wish things were different. If I had the time to give you a fair explanation, then maybe . . ."

"My meeting won't be long. After that I've got all the time in the world."

"But I don't." He traced his hand up my arm and settled it on my shoulder. My body buzzed under his fingers. "There are terms to my plea." He nodded toward the courthouse. "And they include me being on the next plane out of here."

"There's this amazing technology called a phone. You can call me." I wanted to believe that somewhere in the rubble of this mess, there might actually emerge an "us."

He pulled me into him and, wrapping me in the warmth of his embrace, talked softly into my ear. "I can't call you, Samantha."

"The terms of your plea?" I mumbled into his chest.

"Uh huh." His breath tickled through my hair. "But let's be honest. Even if I could, I don't think you'd want to be with me."

I tightened my hold around him and cranked my neck to see his face. "Don't you think you should let me decide that for myself?"

He slid his hands up my back then anchored them on either side of my face. "I've got a pretty good handle on the girl that Sam is, and she's pretty much everything I've ever wanted in a woman. You're smart, and unassuming, and beautiful. And cautious. Too cautious to ever take a chance on a guy like me." He pressed his lips to my forehead, holding the kiss long enough for me to yearn for a real one. Dropping his hands to his sides, he took a step back. "I've got a colorful past, Sam." He shook his head. "I'm not who you think I am."

I felt the void where his hands had just touched my skin. "How do you know who I think you are?" I was trying to sound confident, but the thunderstorm in my gut told me that he'd already made up his mind.

"You think my name is Seth."

"It's not?" Of course it wasn't. Why would he have given me his real name?

He shook his head.

"Then what is it?"

"If I tell you, I might have to kill you." He tried to hold a serious face but quickly lost hold of his grin. I hoped that meant he was going to tell me, but he didn't. Instead he slid his fingers up the base of my neck, laced them through the hair on the back of my head, and lowered his lips to mine. I pressed my body into the firmness of his torso and melted into his kiss. When he pulled away, I buried my head into his chest and held on.

He tilted my head up and looked intently into my eyes. "I want you to use your resources to find out everything you can about me—the real me. Hack into my life, Sam. Dig deep." He touched his thumb to my cheek. "Then, if you're still interested, I'll be waiting."

"I don't think I'm going to find anything that will negate the way I feel." My heart pounded loudly against my chest.

He raised his brow and traced his fingers slowly across my arm as he stepped away. "Trust me," he said. "Make one of your little flow chart things. Analyze everything you find. Really do your homework."

"Fine," I conceded. "And when I'm done with my research, where will I find you?"

"Fishing." He ran his fingertips across my lips then slid into the taxi.

"Could you be more specific?" I urged, still buzzing from his kiss.

"You're a master hacker, Sam. I have no doubt that if you want to find me, you will." With one last, irresistible grin, he snapped the car door closed.

Logic told me to let him disappear on the horizon and move on with my life, but hearts are harder to negotiate with than heads are. If Seth wanted me to dig into his past and hunt him down like some crazed vigilante, I would oblige him. It might take every tool in my bag, but as I clicked my heels briskly across the walkway, my heart soared.

Let the hunt begin.

Thank you for reading HACKED (The Secret of Secrets, Book 1). If you enjoyed what you read, please consider leaving a review on Amazon, Goodreads, and other online book review sites.

Wondering what's next? Need a taste more? Here's a little sample of what awaits Samantha in the next book, HUNTED (The Secret of Secrets, Book 2). Enjoy.

# HUNTED

**The Secret of Secrets, Book 2**

*- The only thing harder than loving a person who is in hiding, is hunting one who doesn't exist.*

# Chapter One

Half of any secret is the knowledge that it exists. The other half – the specifics, the details, and the truths – despite how ugly they might be, is what I was after.

I paused for a moment in front of the courthouse's reflective glass doors and took one last inventory of myself before stepping inside the Federal building. Framed by flowing red locks and an ivory complexion, my blue eyes radiated a surety I'd have been wise to bottle up and store. I'd never been uber-confident in anything beyond my computer screen, but the girl in the glass took each step with calculated, self-assured grandeur.

Is this what Seth saw in me? Some kind of confidence – albeit contrived. Or was it simply the byproduct of how he made me feel? His parting words repeated in my head. "You're a master hacker, Samantha Perry. I have no doubt that if you want to find me, you will."

I gave one last twist to my tailored suit coat then brushed my hands over my hips and down the lines of my penciled skirt. Gulping in the fresh, summer morning air, I pushed past my resurfacing insecurities and pulled the heavy glass door open.

The beauty of Maryland disappeared behind me as the first set of doors snapped closed. A suited man with a silver beard pulled the second door for me then held it open as I walked through. With a curt nod, he went about his business, leaving me alone at the security checkpoint.

"Morning," I said with a forced smile as I dropped my purse in the little bin that was an all too familiar part of any federally-regulated building. The stocky security guard simply nodded as she gave my belongings a push through the x-ray machine then waved me through the security terminal.

The terminal let out a high-pitched beep, alarming the security team that something on my body posed a possible threat. Probably the underwire in my bra, I thought, feeling my previous confidence take a hit. I bit down on my lip and bowed my head toward the floor, unsure if I were more embarrassed for myself or of a government that hadn't figured out that ninety percent of the female population wore wire in their underwear.

An old, burly guard instructed me to spread my legs and pitch my arms out to my side so he could wave a magic little wand over me. Familiar with the drill, I conceded with a sigh. When the wand reached the base of my bosom, it hummed. "It's my bra." I shrugged, unable to look the man in the eye.

"Go ahead," he said bruskly, stepping back to his post with a grin. Undoubtedly his daily routine included frequent brassier incidents. At least one of us seemed to find the humor in the breach of my personal space.

My navy blue heals clicked along the tiled concourse as I swung my purse over my shoulder and made my way to the elevator. The guard may have temporarily put a dent in my dignity, but not even a full pat down could've killed the buzz Seth had instigated within me.

The elevator chimed with each floor it ascended. I counted each ding – six before the lift stopped. The door slid open and, with a deep breath, I stepped back on solid ground.

"Can I help you?" The reception counter sat across the vestibule from the elevator. It was so tall I could barely see the face behind the voice. I took a few steps closer before I got a good glance at the small, very serious-looking woman. Her dark hair was slicked back in a tight bun and her left brow – penciled to perfection – was raised to a discerning point.

"I have a meeting with Mr. Jasper Banks." I'd made a mental note not to laugh at his name, though it sounded antiquated at best and serial killer-ish at worst. After spending several months under an alias derived simply from the color of my hair, I wasn't in the position to judge. At least Jasper had some semblance of respectability. I couldn't say the same about my alter ego, Ginger.

"Are you Samantha Perry?"

"Yes." I nodded.

"From the NSA?" She raised her brow even higher.

"Yes." I nodded for a second time. Was she expecting another?

"Mr. Banks is finishing up with his previous appointment." She motioned toward a bench along the edge of the corridor. "If you'd like to have a seat, he will be with you in a minute."

I sat on the hard wooden bench and crossed my ankles, then traced my eyes over the patterns of the marble floor. My fingers began to fidget nervously on my lap. I wasn't exactly looking forward to my interview with Mr. Banks. If I'd wanted to deal with lawyers, I'd have studied law, not cyber security.

Moments after my fingers had found a comfortable tapping rhythm on my leg, Mr. Banks' door swung open and two men exited together. "Thank you again, Mr. Carey." The man's voice was low and daunting. I wondered how many cases he won simply through intimidation. Maybe that's why he'd been chosen to represent the federal government in the PumpPurge Case. And maybe he was the reason Seth had been motivated to leave so hastily. "Miss Perry?" He sternly looked my way.

I stood quickly and brushed the non-existent wrinkles out of my skirt. "Yes." I fumbled, suddenly more nervous than I'd anticipated.

"Please come in." Mr. Banks held the door open and nodded in the direction of his office. Subtle gray pinstripes and a flashy red tie added a touch of interest to his otherwise conservative black suit. Almost instinctually, my confidence cowered and my gaze fell to the ground. Brown loafers, about the same color as his thinning head of hair, anchored his feet to the tiled floor.

"Hi, Sama…" The second man started as we passed each other. "I mean, Miss Perry."

I'd been so frazzled by Mr. Banks authoritative presentation that I hadn't paid a lot of attention to the man exiting the room with him. "Samantha is fine." I forced a smile at my coworker, David Carey, though pleasantries weren't typically part of my modus operandi. "How are you, David?" Of all the people I'd worked with in the Maryland NSA division, David was the closest to my age – somewhere in his mid to upper twenties, I'd guess, though his hair had already begun to thin on top.

He pushed his suit coat aside and stuffed his hands into the front pockets of his trousers. His shoulders rolled forward and he looked timidly at the ground. "Good," he said haltingly, as if he held his breath.

"Good." I gave him a curt nod then shifted my attention back toward the beckoning office beyond Mr. Banks.

I heard David take a few hesitant steps before the sound of his shoes on the marble came to a halt behind me. "I'm glad you're not really dead." The comment was as awkward as his stuttered, muffled delivery.

"Yeah, me too," I said, turning to give him a smile.

He offered a brief, awkward smile of his own then quickly adjusted his vision back down to the floor, sealing our fumbled conversation with his silence. Before I'd been assigned a new identity and shipped off to Utah, David and I had spent a year with our workstations next to each other. One might think we'd have developed a friendship over that time, but when you put two introverted cyber geeks in the same room, they talk about algorithms and codes and keep socializing to a minimum.

I didn't wait for David to walk away before turning my attention back to Mr. Banks. He firmly shook my hand and offered me a surprisingly warm smile. "A few of my colleagues will be joining us," he said as he invited me into his office.

"Okay." I stepped toward the richly decorated room with as much confidence as I could muster. It wasn't like I harbored any deep secrets from the government. Not about the details of 43M – aka PumpPurge – anyway. Suddenly I wondered what David had to offer to the case. Though we hadn't seen each other in nearly five months, I'd sent him confidential emails to which he never responded. I assumed Rushton, the mastermind behind PumpPurge, had prevented them from getting through. Maybe I'd assumed wrong.

I cast my eyes back toward the waiting area. The elevator chimed its arrival and, as if on cue, David glanced over his shoulder. Our eyes met for a brief, awkward moment then he turned abruptly and tripped his way into the elevator box.

Though I was measurably more confident than David – at least in the sense that I could successfully put one foot in front of the other in a somewhat graceful manner – Mr. Banks picked up on my uneasiness. "I promise we don't bite," he said, his face contorting into a somewhat one-sided smile.

"I'll take your word on it," I replied with a half-smile of my own, though I doubted I'd ever take anyone's word on anything again.

To continue reading HUNTED (The Secret of Secrets, Book 2), swing by Amazon or http://www.stephanieworlton.com/

ACKNOWLEDGEMENTS:

To the readers who loved and embraced *The Secret of Secrets, HACKED* series in their original format as novellas, thank you for nudging me to write the full story.

To my beta readers, you are my saving grace. Thanks for always being willing to help.

And to my amazing author friends (especially Stacy for dragging me to the cabin and forcing me to make words!) You peeps continually encourage and push me. It truly takes a village and I'm honored to be a part of yours.

# ABOUT THE AUTHOR

Stephanie lives in the shadow of the Rocky Mountains where she enjoys frequent opportunities to observe nature and feed her creative spirit. In addition to writing, she spends her days designing, building, painting, drawing, landscaping, and snuggling with her dogs. She has her own collection of power tools, a plethora of camera equipment, and a passion for shoes.

**Connect with Stephanie online**
Facebook @AuthorStephanieWorlton
www.stephanieworlton.com
Amazon Author Page
Goodreads Author Page

## OTHER BOOKS BY STEPHANIE:

*HUNTED (The Secret of Secrets, Book 2)* - The only thing harder than loving a person who is in hiding, is hunting one who doesn't exist.

*HOOKED, the final HACK (The Secret of Secrets, Book 3)* - Spontaneity is so far out of Samantha Perry's comfort zone, even the thought of it gives her anxiety. But love makes a girl – even a typically contemplative and logical one – do things she wouldn't normally do.

*Hope's Journey* - High school seniors, Sydney and Alex think they have life all figured out, until one decision turns their plans upside down. Faced with pending parenthood, they must learn to forgive each other – and themselves – if they have any hope of moving on.

*All the Finer Things* - Megan Hamilton's posh life, designer clothes, and stunning penthouse leave her wanting for nothing . . . or do they? Controlled by his obsessive pursuit of perfection, Doctor Matthew Hamilton will stop nothing short of breaking his young, spirited bride into a subservient trophy wife. How far will Megan have to go to escape Matt's obsessive control and abuse? And how much will she have to lose before she gets there?

## AUTHOR'S NOTE:

In the fall of 2014, I sat in our family car, roaring southbound down I-15 on a little road trip. As the Utah scenery zipped by our windows, I excitedly told my husband about an upcoming anthology publication I'd been considering submitting something to. The catch was two-fold: first, I had to come up with an idea that fit within the parameters of the publication. They were looking for romances based on the concept of "secret identities." And, second, the story could only be 15,000 words. That, for me, is an incredibly *short* story. (I'd never published anything under 90,000 words before!)

We had a good laugh about the absurdity of me writing something so short – I am, after all, a wordy kind of girl – and then we started brainstorming ideas. By the end of our trip, my hubby and I had outlined the entirety of Samantha's story. Two weeks later, I finished the first draft of HACKED and submitted it to the anthology.

HACKED was original published in early 2015 as part of the Sweet & Sassy Anthology's Hidden Identities Collection. Several months later it was released on its own as the opening story in The Secret of Secret novella series.

All three books in the series went on to earn best-seller status as short reads. After two years of nudging from my author friends as well as my readers, I decided to do Sam's story justice and fill in the details that had to be skipped the first time around.

I hope you enjoyed reading the full-version of HACKED as much as I enjoyed writing it.